For

JEANETTE GREAVES

FIGHT FOR THE FUTURE

RANSOMED HEARTS, PART ONE

This is a work of fiction. Names, characters, places, and incidents either are the product of the author's imagination or are used fictitiously. Any resemblance to actual persons, living or dead, events, or locales is entirely coincidental.

Copyright © 2021 by Jeanette Greaves
www.bloginbasket.com

Published by
Bardale Press

All rights reserved. No part of this book may be reproduced or used in any manner without written permission of the copyright owner except for the use of quotations in a book review

Cover by Ravven
www.ravven.com

First paperback edition 2021

Chapter 1

The single-decker bus coughed its way through the valleys of north Lancashire, leaving behind a gentle trail of smoke in the hot summer air. Two young men sat quietly on opposite ends of the back seat, their eyes alert and watchful, taking in all that was new to them. Between them, firmly restrained against the bumps and jolts, were two guitar cases.

Their destination was the village of Bardale, miles from everywhere, the route's terminus, and, perhaps, a safe place. The two passengers exchanged wary glances as the bus finally rolled to a halt next to a small village green.

'Reet, lads, we're here,' confirmed the driver, putting on the handbrake and reaching for his cigarettes.

Anthony adopted the air of an older brother, shook his head, and turned to retrieve their luggage from the overhead rack. Reaching the platform, he threw one of the thin suitcases at his twin. Tomas caught it without dropping his precious guitar.

Anthony jumped off the platform and thanked the bus driver, who nodded abruptly and opened his newspaper.

The brothers looked around. The village was noisy with the sounds of children playing. Few adults were visible. The two pubs on either side of the green were both shut. Anthony winked at his brother. 'The Black Dog or the White Bull?' he enquired.

'I guess it'll have to be the Black Dog,' Tomas said. They made their way to the back of the pub. The back door and windows were all wide open, the building hungry for the slightest breeze. Anthony stepped forwards and knocked gently on the door. 'Hello, anyone in?' he called out, his voice carrying deep into the house.

A birdlike woman bustled to the door, wiping wet hands on her white apron. She looked the young men up and down. Anthony waited for her judgement, aware that he needed a haircut, aware that he looked young and poorly dressed. She seemed to come to a decision.

'I'm Mrs Martin, the landlady. Can I help you boys?' she asked.

Tomas nodded. 'Yes, ma'am, we're visiting from France, and looking for somewhere to stay. Do you have a room?'

'Aye, just the one bed, mind, but you're obviously brothers, so that's fine, I expect. How long were you planning on staying?'

Anthony spoke up. 'At least a week, maybe longer.'

She nodded. She'd find out later what they were here for. She named a price, and noted how the brothers looked at each other before agreeing. 'I'll show you up to the room then.'

They followed her through the large clean kitchen, and upstairs. The family living quarters were on one long corridor. A smaller corridor, at right angles to it, had four rooms coming off it.

'The bathroom's at the end, there'll be some warm water, but don't go mad with it. We've put in a shower, it's quicker in the mornings. You'll get the hang of it,' she said with some pride. 'And keep quiet with them guitars, the other guests work for a living and need their sleep.'

The brothers agreed readily, lugged their bags and guitars into the room and started to unpack, laying their scant possessions out neatly. They each had a much-needed lukewarm shower, shaved, and gave each other a haircut before going downstairs. The pub had just opened, and they stopped at the bar. It looked like breakfast would be something to look forward to, but they would have to make their own arrangements for other meals. Mrs Martin directed them to the chippy, which would be open until nine o'clock. Anthony smiled; he loved England for its good solid food that didn't let you forget that you'd just eaten. They were hungry, and headed straight for the chippy, drawn by the scent of fish and vinegar.

The woman behind the counter was looking bored until they walked in, but she straightened up and smiled when she saw them. To Anthony's amusement, she served them fish, chips, and a barrage of questions that established that they were intending to stay for at least a week, that they intended to eat every night at the chip shop, and that they were indeed single and completely unspoken for.

It was cooler by the river, where Anthony and Tomas found a patch of shaded grassy bank and settled down to eat their meal out of the newspaper. They were quiet, no need for words, as they watched the low river swirl over the dark rocks. As the day cooled into evening, they made their way back to the pub, ordered two pints and took a table by the bar.

Before too long, the landlord took a seat at their table. He was a tall, broad man in his fifties, his greying hair was slicked back with Brylcreem, and he wore tweed trousers, a white shirt, and a tweed waistcoat that stretched with rigid determination across his belly.

'Hello, lads, you're staying round here for a while, eh? What brings you to Bardale?'

Tomas glanced at his brother, cautiously waiting for his lead. Anthony pushed his fingers through his hair and looked up. 'Well, our great-grandma came from this part of the world, and our ma always wanted us to come and see it. Grandma Margaret talked so much about northern England, and how beautiful it was. So we decided to come here and see for ourselves.'

The landlord lifted his tankard, drained it, and wiped his lips. 'Well lads, is it what you expected?'

Anthony nodded, a sudden smile lighting up his face. 'It is. Maybe it's the beautiful warm day, but I think this place, this valley, is charming.'

The landlord gazed at him for a while longer. Anthony was suddenly aware that several of the local women were glancing in his direction too. He turned off the smile; he'd learned that it brought attention, and he wasn't ready for too much of that quite yet.

Tomas stood and made his way to the bar, ordering another round. The landlady took his money and smiled. 'I'll bring the drinks over, seeing

Fight for the Future

as it's your first night here.'

By the time the twins had gone to an early bed, they had let it be known that they were distantly connected with the village, that they were not wealthy tourists, just young men looking for jobs, and that they loved music. They lay awake quietly, listening to the low murmuring of gossip in the pub below them.

Tomas sat up and switched on the light. He reached over to his jacket and took a small piece of paper from the inside pocket. He unfolded it. Anthony sat up, frowning.

'Tomas, we agreed we'd destroy it.'

'I know, but I miss them,' his brother said, his voice low. 'Mum and Dad, Sylvia and Audrey.'

'Read it once more, then rip it up. I'll put it in the fire tomorrow.' Anthony's voice was firm, and Tomas looked from his brother's face to the grubby, much-read scrap of paper. Then he read it one last time.

'Dear Sons, all is well. We're all fighting fit, and keeping the wolf from the door. We hope that you are well. All our love. The Family.' Tomas looked at the precise, cramped handwriting again, written with heavily blotted black ink. He could almost see his mother labouring over the paper, using English rather than their native French dialect. The next letter would be from his father. He or his brother would go to pick it up from the delivery address in Manchester that they'd cautiously set up.

They'd already replied to this letter, taking a train out from Manchester on a branch line, getting off at a random stop, walking for ten miles, posting the letter, and returning immediately. 'We love you, we miss you, we're fine.' That was all it said. It was all they *dared* say.

'Do you think we'll find any of our kind here?' whispered Tomas. Anthony stared into space; it was too much to hope for. Tomorrow they would start to investigate the history of the village, and discover the names and fates of their distant cousins.

The next day the twins started to explore. Within an hour they'd found two or three big houses, a small council estate of about a dozen semi-detached houses, and four or five cramped streets of terraced cottages. The centre of the village held the two pubs, the green which lay between them, a post office next to the shop, and the chippy. The village didn't spill across the river, and the bridge took the road southwards. On the other side of the village, a chapel sat back on the hillside. The modest detached house next to it was the vicarage. A new wooden-sided village hall stood uncertainly just outside the village, a building that was just learning its role, judging from the assortment of notices pinned to the board outside. Apart from the newish council estate and village hall, it was what they'd been told to expect. They planned to explore further at another time, visiting places familiar from old stories – stories of happiness, and stories of horror too.

The twins bought sliced bread, cold meat, and bottled pop from the little shop, and recklessly splurged a little of their hard-saved cash on a bag of brightly coloured liquorice torpedoes. The shopkeeper noted their politeness, having already heard about the strangers in town.

'On holiday, are you?' she enquired.

'In a way, but we might stay a while if we can find work,' Anthony answered. 'Is there much work around here?'

'Oh, there's always some farmer somewhere who needs help. You look like strong lads. Where did you say you were from?'

'Europe,' said Anthony firmly, refusing to be more specific. 'But our great-grandmother lived round here.'

'And what was her name?'

Anthony shrugged. 'Mum's mum's mum – we don't know her surname, just her stories. She was a Sally.'

'Lots of Sallys round here,' said the shopkeeper, handing him his change. They headed out of town, finding a footpath into the hills and hiking up until they reached a spot that gave a good view of the village, the valley, and the roads into and out of it.

'What do you think?' asked Tomas, settling down on a boulder and laying slices of boiled ham on to bread.

'Too early to say…' His brother trailed off, alert, watchful. 'Who's that?' he called. He'd heard something. He headed for the low stone wall that ran just below the brow of the hill, and peered over it.

'I say, can't you find your own hill?' said a

ruffled young man, who was clearly enjoying the company of his girlfriend. Anthony was ready to apologise, but Tomas was already by his side, looking over the wall. The girl didn't have that tired look most of the village women seemed to wear. She had brilliant dark-brown eyes, long dishevelled chestnut curls and, from what he could see, a lush figure that had left girlhood behind and laid firm claim on womanhood.

Tomas sketched a little bow. 'I doubt we'd ever find another hill with such a wonderful view,' he said, straight-faced. The young man stood up, furious, but Anthony placated him with a hand on his shoulder.

'Forgive my brother, he's a little too honest sometimes. My apologies. I'm Anthony, this is Tomas…'

The young man glared. 'Jennison. Frederick Jennison. I'm the doctor's son.' The girl stood up, smoothing her skirt down and adjusting her blouse. 'I'm Miriam Hartnell,' she said, flashing an annoyed look at Jennison. 'Freddie, we may not be in your fashionable circles, but a gentleman should introduce a lady.'

Mr Jennison scowled. 'May I present Miss Hartnell, my fiancée.'

Anthony took her hand, bowed and kissed it. 'Charmed.'

Jennison flushed further, and took her other hand, pulling her away. 'We're going back, we're late.'

'What are we late for?' she protested,

looking back as he pulled her away.

'Never mind,' he growled.

The twins watched soberly as the couple made their way down the path, towards the village.

'Fiancée?' Tomas said sadly.

'Yes. Not wife,' said Anthony with a grin. 'Anyway, we're not after making trouble, are we? Leave her alone. For now. Who knows, she could be what we're looking for.'

His brother favoured him with a cynical look. 'Charmed?' he snorted. 'Come on, let's have lunch, I'm starving.'

Chapter 2

'Does this ever feel cold-blooded to you?'

Tomas looked up from his guitar and gazed quizzically at his twin.

'What? Music? Never,' he replied.

Anthony frowned, wondering if identical twins could have vastly different intelligence levels. 'No, stupid. I mean this ... this trawling through family trees.' He was sitting on the window ledge of their bedroom, puzzling over pencilled-in notes in a rough paper jotter.

Tomas shrugged. 'Find me a pretty girl, and I'm sure my blood will warm up.' He winked at his brother, and returned his attention to his guitar. He cleared his throat and started to strum, his low, clear voice earnestly singing out the first few steps of 'Three Steps to Heaven'.

His brother looked at him in mock despair. 'Tomas, remember that girl on the hill?'

'Miriam Hartnell? Rose Queen for three years in succession? Bride-to-be of the doctor's son?' Tomas's gaze rested on the roses printed on the faded wallpaper.

'You do remember then? And you've obviously done your research. Well, she's on the list.' Anthony watched his brother, waiting for a reaction.

'That's nice.' Tomas smiled dreamily, then refocused. 'She's on the list? She can't be! OK, she's a descendant, but I thought we'd established that her mother died in an accident.'

Anthony bit into the end of the pencil,

looking thoughtfully at his brother. 'I've widened the search. The fact that the mother died in an accident doesn't mean that she wasn't a half-blood, it just means that we don't have any real indication that she *was*. But then again, we don't have any indication that she *wasn't*, do we? And Miriam *is* an only child...'

'Miriam has an older brother,' Tomas pointed out. 'Half-blood women don't often have more than one child.'

Anthony smiled smugly. 'He's adopted. I bought him a pint or two last night, we got chatting, it came out in conversation.'

'Ah,' said Tomas. 'So now what?'

'Well, we have several possibles, but only two of them are in the right age group and unmarried – Linda Lucas and Miriam Hartnell. Linda's not seeing anyone, according to the gossip, and Miriam is engaged. I suggest we try to detach Miriam from Jennison. If it works, we'll let her decide which one of us she likes, and the other one courts Linda. What do you think?'

'I think Linda's a cold fish, but we're short of options. What if we break up Miriam and Jennison, then find out she's not what we want?' There was a note of uncertainty in Tomas's voice.

Anthony studied the ceiling. 'What if we decide not to think about how badly we're behaving, and just get on with what we came here to do – find half-blood women and marry them?'

Tomas bit his lip, and returned his attention to his guitar and his singing. He refused to look up when Anthony sighed in exasperation.

Later that evening, Anthony leaned against the wall of the bridge, watching the clear stream follow its long defined path. He was aware of Tomas approaching, given away by the scent of vinegar and damp paper. 'Chips again, but I managed to scrounge some batter scraps,' Tomas bragged. 'Oh, and I've got a trial for a job – building. I start tomorrow.'

Anthony cheered up. 'That's great. But when did you ever build anything?'

Tomas laughed. 'Well, so far as my new boss is concerned, I'm an experienced labourer but, being foreign, I've no references. I played up the French accent a bit. He's desperate, and he just wants someone to lift and carry for now. I can do that. The pay's OK, we can afford fish or pudding every night now.'

Tomas's job left Anthony alone during the day. He spent as much time as possible in the village, chatting to new friends and strangers, listening to the stories they were happy to tell to a new ear. A week or so after Tomas found work, Anthony was cheerfully making himself useful in the pub by changing a barrel. He emerged from the cellar to see a different face in the pub. It was hard to judge his age. He could have been anything between thirty and fifty; lines of worry marked his face, but he had the sleek, jet-black hair of a young man. As if he felt Anthony's gaze, the stranger returned the stare, stood, and walked to the bar.

'You're the new lad round 'ere.' It wasn't a

question.

'One of them,' Anthony returned. 'Anthony Preston.'

The man shook his head. 'Preston? Hmm. Well, what tha calls thaself isn't my business. I hear you're looking for work.'

Anthony was cautious. The man looked like he hadn't had a decent night's sleep for a long time. 'Yes, I am. Are you hiring?'

The stranger shrugged. 'It's time I did.' He extended a sun-browned arm, tightly corded with the kind of muscle that comes from hard labour. 'I'm Eddie Shepherd, I'm looking for a farmhand. I'll warn you, I've got a reputation for being hard to work with.'

Anthony summoned his most devastating smile. 'I'm pretty easy to work with, I've been told, so maybe we're a good match. I've done farm work before.'

'Round here?'

'No, back home in France. No references, you'll have to take my word.'

'I'll do that. Six tomorrow morning, at the farmhouse. The Shepherd farm. Mrs Martin can tell you how to get there.'

Eddie Shepherd turned and walked out, leaving the best part of a pint on the table.

The Shepherd farm was bigger than Anthony had expected, and disturbingly quiet. He'd arrived at ten to six, and had been shown the outside tap, for drinking water, and given a pair of dirty and battered

Jeanette Greaves

overalls, which he welcomed.

'Day labourer rate, until I know what you can do,' Eddie had said quietly. 'If I say so, you're off the farm, no arguments.'

'No arguments.' Anthony nodded. 'What's first?'

'Well, t'milking's done, so it's time for breakfast. We'll eat in the kitchen. Bacon and eggs. I know you were out too early for breakfast at the Dog, and a man needs to eat.'

They had a small, elderly terrier for company. He stayed close to Eddie, and kept a watchful eye on Anthony. 'That's a good dog." Anthony said.

'Ratter,' Eddie said, then shook his head. 'Well, retired ratter, he catches the odd little 'un, now and again ... but not a pet. This is a farm, no room for pets.'

Anthony watched as Eddie's hand crept down to caress the terrier's ears, and he kept quiet.

Anthony had hoped for a tour of the farm, but had spent the whole day in one of the outlying fields, laying a hedge that had been neglected for a couple of years. He wrapped some sacking round his hands as he chopped, bent and twisted the cut stems of hawthorn, beech and holly. He'd end up scratched to bits, but he healed fast, and he didn't mind. It was five by the time he got back.

'Hedge done?' Eddie asked.

'Three quarters done. There's no animals in that field, so I thought the rest would wait. I'll finish it tonight if you like...' Anthony waited.

'Three quarters is more than I expected. Get home wi' you. Here's your wages, and a cheese butty to be getting on with.' Eddie scowled. 'Leftovers, I wasn't that hungry. Oh, and bring gloves tomorrow, you daft bugger.'

He turned towards the farmhouse. 'Hang on, my daughter's shouting summat.'

He walked in, and five minutes later came out again, carrying a pair of worn canvas gloves. 'Seems it's my job to provide you with gloves. Here you go.' He was almost smiling. Anthony took the gloves and nodded, then made his way back to the pub. Tomas was already back, and waiting to hear about Anthony's day.

'Big farm, bigger than you'd think. Eddie owns it, which surprised me, he doesn't act like a landowner type. Mostly wheat and winter veg, small orchard, small dairy herd and a milking shed. Ducks on the pond, but for home consumption, I reckon. Chickens for eggs and for home use. I think he sells the surplus but he's not farming them seriously. It looks like nothing's been done on the farm for a year. Don't know why, he seems like a hard worker. Maybe he's been ill. One daughter, who I didn't see. No sign of a wife.'

Tomas nodded. 'We'll get the gossip eventually. Will he keep you on?'

'He's told me to come back tomorrow.' Anthony grinned. 'I reckon I'm hired.'

Chapter 3

The twins found out when the local folk nights were, taking their guitars along and learning the songs, finding some of them familiar, passed down in their own family from their great-grandmother. Day by day, they settled into the village, eating and drinking in different places, chatting to the old folk in the pub at night. They hiked in the hills during their free time, to stretch their legs and exhaust themselves as much as possible, to mask their growing restlessness and urge to change and run together. They had a fright when Mrs Martin jokingly asked them when they slept; she knew they helped tidy the pub every night, but were still up early every morning for work. It would be unwise to get a reputation for not needing much sleep. They cut back on their pub nights, staying in their room two or three evenings a week, bored and frustrated, whiling away their wakefulness with silent research and whispered conversations.

Anthony talked about the future, imagining two families growing side by side. Tomas spoke of their younger sisters back home, Sylvia and Audrey, and the threat to them and their parents. Anthony was more positive; their parents had raised many children, and knew how to keep their youngest safe. The twins talked about Miriam – both of them were fascinated by her, amused by her innocent self-assurance.

'They're the golden couple, she and Jennison,' Anthony said wistfully. 'Mr Martin told me that Jennison's dad is a doctor, down near Lancaster.

Plenty of money, and Jennison is studying medicine too. Everyone reckons he's a catch for a village lass like Miriam. Jennison's grandad has a title, they reckon.'

'The English are weird.' Tomas shrugged. 'So, he has a so-called noble ancestor, and will have money. Miriam needs more than that, she needs passion. Jennison walks around with her like she's the lucky one. He is crazy. He cannot see what he has.'

'She's pretty enough, but what else do we know about her?' Anthony bit his lip. 'Mr Martin says —'

'Oh, hush with your old gossip.' Tomas wriggled on the bed, making a bid for more space. Anthony, long practised in this manoeuvre, wriggled back and smothered a giggle.

'Yeah well, Mr Martin told me that Miriam's dad is the local magistrate, and that he doesn't want Miriam to have a job. She just has to organise his social life and look pretty.' Anthony tried to sound dismissive, but in the face of Tomas's amused silence he gave up. 'OK, so she looks very nice. And from what I hear she gets on OK with her dad. They've got one of those big houses on the road out of the village. We should check it out sometime…' He glanced across and rolled his eyes. Tomas was drowsy, at last. Anthony, bored, matched his brother's rhythmic breathing and was soon asleep too.

They studied Miriam's comings and goings. She was usually seen in the company of several girls of her own age, or with Freddie Jennison. Anthony and Tomas worked out Jennison's schedule: he was always punctual in his visits, and the twins managed to be walking past the Hartnell house at the time that he arrived and departed. After a week of this, Tomas was rewarded by a friendly wave from Miriam as she opened the door to Freddie. Her fiancé looked around and scowled when he saw the young man smiling back. That night, Anthony didn't see him leave at his usual time, and found out the next morning that Jennison had sulked his way into the White Bull barely an hour after being admitted to Miriam's home.

The following Friday night, Jennison led Miriam into the Black Dog to enjoy the usual evening of local folk music. He frowned when he saw that the twins were playing and singing, and engineered things so that he could keep his eye on them, and Miriam had her back to them. At half past nine, a group of Miriam's friends from the next village arrived. A couple of the girls started to complain good-naturedly about the music to the landlady. Mrs Martin laughed, and asked if any of the musicians knew anything a little more up to date. Anthony and Tomas looked around. The other players didn't seem to mind, so they started to play 'Three Steps to Heaven', to eager applause from the girls. Miriam moved her chair round to watch, and Tomas winked at her. Jennison saw the wink, and flushed.

Anthony introduced himself and Tomas as 'The Preston Brothers ... no relation to Johnny Preston!' The younger crowd laughed. Anthony started to sing 'Cathy's Clown'. One of the girls squealed in delight. 'My name's Cathy!' she called out to him, and he favoured her with a delicious smile.

They decided that two numbers were enough, and switched to 'My Old Man's a Dustman.' The rest of the musicians joined in. The regulars joined in with the singalong, and Tomas put his guitar down and went to the bar. Jennison jumped up, pushing past Miriam and making his way to the bar.

'What do you think you're playing at?' he enquired, flushed and angry.

Tomas took a sip of his beer, and turned. 'It's just a bit of fun, don't you like music?'

'I don't mean the music, I mean the way you were winking at my fiancée!' spluttered Jennison.

Tomas shrugged. 'I was winking at the girls, none in particular. It's part of the show,' he said casually, turning back to his pint.

Anthony watched carefully, then put his own guitar down and made his way over to the girls. A group of young men had caught up with them, and had joined in with the chat. Anthony stood for a moment, smiling, waiting to be invited to sit down. A smiling, half-drunk farmhand, with wild ginger curls, signalled for him to take the empty corner seat, which had been occupied by Jennison. Anthony demurred, pointing out that it was taken, and Miriam stood up and moved over into Jennison's place.

'He won't mind *me* taking his seat, will he? And you can take my chair. There! All settled.' She looked round at her friends as if she'd solved the world's problems single-handedly, and they smiled back.

Anthony introduced himself, and started to get to know Miriam's friends, glancing back now and again to keep an eye on the bar, where Freddie Jennison was impatiently trying to get the attention of the busy bar staff. Tomas smiled at Mrs Martin, and offered to help. She flashed him a grateful smile, and he ducked behind the bar, going straight to Jennison.

'Can I help you?' he said, innocently.

Jennison glared at him. 'Pint. And a Babycham.'

'For your pretty young lady...' Tomas laughed, pulling a pint, and opening a bottle of Babycham while it settled.

'I'd appreciate it if you didn't say anything else about my fiancée,' said Jennison stiffly. 'It was dreadfully rude of you to speak to her when you saw us on the hill.'

Tomas looked across the pub, his eyes dramatically wide open. 'That's the same girl? Good grief! I didn't recognise her so dressed up. I'm sorry.'

Increasingly annoyed, Jennison turned to look at Miriam, and frowned when he saw her deep in conversation with Anthony, Cathy, and the red-haired farmhand. He strode across the pub.

'We're leaving,' he said.

'Why?'

'This place is going downhill, they'll let any riff-raff in,' he said, scowling.

Tomas came over, carrying a pint and a Babycham.

Fight for the Future

'Mr Jennison, you've forgotten your drinks.' He bowed a little as he set Miriam's drink down, leaning over his brother's shoulder. The two of them looked at her at the same time, the same smile, the same 'Isn't this fun?' expression. She couldn't help but smile back, and her fiancé's face went pale.

'Miriam, are you coming or not?'

She looked at him, and at her friends, who were falling quiet.

'I can feel a headache coming on, actually,' she said with a frown. 'Maybe you should walk me back home.' She stood, and slipped out from behind the table, pushing close past the twins. Jennison seized her hand and almost dragged her behind him out of the door. As she left, she looked back. Tomas and Anthony were already chatting to her friends, but Tomas looked up, a fraction of a second before he was out of her sight, and winked once more.

Anthony glanced at Tomas, and whispered, 'What did we do?'

Tomas shrugged. 'She didn't want a scene, don't worry about it. It's Jennison she's angry with.'

He looked for a moment at the drinks that he had brought over.

'Well, these are paid for. Cathy? Do you like Babycham, or do I have to drink it myself?' The girl giggled, and accepted the drink.

Over the next few weeks, the twins made themselves at home with the group of friends. Anthony identified the redhead, Nick, as the clown of the group, and subtly fed him a series of 'affectionate'

Jeanette Greaves

nicknames for Jennison, which Nick proceeded to take full credit for. Even Miriam giggled when Nick looked up, wide-eyed, and informed the group that 'The Fun Prevention Officer' had arrived.

One evening, pushed too far yet again, Jennison rose and declared that he was leaving. The group teased him good-naturedly, until he took hold of Miriam's arm and started to drag her up. She protested, and Anthony stood up. 'That's not how a gentleman behaves,' he said quietly.

Miriam pulled herself away and scowled. 'No, he's right, Freddie. I've had enough of your jealousy. We're just having a laugh, all of us. Get over it.'

'You and your laughs! I should have known you couldn't be trusted. You never did put up much of a fight, did you?' said Jennison, bitterly. The crowd went quiet, Miriam paled, and Nick stood up.

'Freddie, take that back,' he suggested mildly. Freddie looked around. Tomas and Anthony had moved gracefully away from the table, and were looking at him as if he'd crawled from under a stone. Cathy was hugging Miriam, who was sitting perfectly still.

Jennison nodded. 'I see, you're all siding with the wops,' he muttered.

Tomas smiled dangerously. 'Frogs, not wops,' he said. There was nervous laughter from the table. Behind the bar, Mr Martin watched carefully.

Jennison swallowed. 'Miriam, I apologise. Now will you come with me?'

'I don't think so,' she said clearly. The young man stood for a moment, bright red with embarrassment and anger, before turning on his heel and storming out. Miriam stood and walked into the ladies' toilets, closely followed by Cathy. The group tried to start chatting again, but gradually went quiet, drifting off in ones and twos. When Cathy and Miriam came out, Miriam was carefully and freshly made up. Nick was waiting patiently. 'Come on Cathy, let's go. Miriam, shall we walk you home?' She nodded, turning to smile weakly at Tomas and Anthony as she left.

The following Monday, Anthony had driven up to the shop with some eggs from the farm. Miriam was choosing biscuits from the boxes at the side of the shop. He noticed that she was no longer wearing her engagement ring, and after he'd been paid for the eggs, and bought matches and flour for Eddie, he sat outside, waiting. She smiled weakly at him.

'Do you want to talk?' he said.

'I'd rather disappear quietly,' she confided.

'Why?'

'Oh, I get the feeling that everyone is talking about me. They all said it wouldn't work out, that I was too fast for Frederick, but I thought we were OK. Then he started getting all possessive. I don't know what came over him. It seems that when Tomas turned up, it was like a red rag to a bull.'

'Tomas, eh?' Anthony smiled wryly.

'Oh, and you too, of course, he doesn't like either of you. I think it goes back to when you ... you know ... on the hill.'

'When we were in the wrong place at the

wrong time? I'm sorry about that.'

'No, it wasn't your fault,' she said, gazing at the river.

Anthony looked away. It *had* been his fault, almost entirely – but, then again, nobody had forced Jennison into behaving the way he did. In a way, he'd done Miriam a favour; she and the doctor's son were clearly unsuited to each other.

She gave a little laugh. 'I was a silly girl. I just wanted to get married and leave home. It didn't seem to matter who to. And then Freddie said we'd have a long engagement, and we weren't getting married for another four years!'

'He's daft,' Anthony told her. 'If I had a girl like you, I wouldn't put anything off.'

She stood up, smiling. 'Enough flirting, young man. I'm supposed to be mourning a good match. I don't suppose Tomas will be in the pub at all this week?'

'Friday night is folk night,' sighed Anthony.

'I'll be there. With the crowd,' she said, standing up and walking home, head high.

Anthony drove back to the farm, not quite as disappointed as he'd expected to be. So, it was Tomas. He could live with that. That night, he saw Linda outside the chip shop, and invited her to go to the cinema with him on Friday night.

Two nervous young men sat on their bed on Friday evening. They'd each made the most of the weak shower, scraping a shave and washing their hair. They'd mixed and matched their meagre wardrobes, decided that they looked good enough, and sat looking at each other.

Anthony spoke first. 'Remind me why we're doing this?'

Tomas laughed. 'Because Mama told us to?'

'Remind me why we're doing this?' Anthony repeated.

'For the family,' said Tomas solemnly. 'To survive.'

Anthony swallowed. 'I just wish the three kinds of women smelled different, or looked different. Anything would help! Instead, we have to guess. You'd think we'd be able to tell, somehow…'

Tomas shrugged. 'If there was a woman like us, and she was changing, and running, we would pick up her scent if we changed...'

Anthony swore. 'But we can't run, we can't change. It's just too risky. Mama made that quite clear. As it stands, we could easily tie ourselves down to the wrong women completely.'

His brother stood and looked out of the window. 'Miriam? The wrong woman? I can't see how that could ever be possible.'

'Oh, shut up, she's got no taste in men, for a start,' said Anthony, resigned. He checked his reflection in the mirror once more, brushing his hair back a little. 'I look too bloody young. She'll never take me seriously.' Linda was six years his senior, although that wasn't something that Anthony planned on telling her that night.

'Relax! Look, I'm going downstairs now, it sounds like Miriam's gang have arrived. At least you have a date. All I have is a vague understanding that we'll be in the same room at the same time.'

'Oh, believe me, I know that look. She's interested in you.' Anthony looked out of the window. 'Right, I'm off too. I'll go out the back door. I'll see you later.'

Tomas made his way downstairs, joining the ad hoc group of musicians. He chatted to a couple who had driven from Lancaster to listen to 'the foreign guitarists', and kept his eye on the group in the corner. Miriam was quieter than usual, sitting between two of her friends. Every so often she would look across at him and smile. The night crawled by, some of the tunes were execrable, others were fun and Tomas got into them, playing around with the melody a little. He demurred when asked to sing something 'more modern', claiming that he was shy without his brother. At last, the night came to an end, and people started to drift home.

Nick, Cathy and Miriam were the last of the crowd to leave. Tomas was helping out, picking up empty glasses and taking them to the bar. Miriam turned to him. 'Tom, Nick's got an early start tomorrow, and he and Cathy live in the opposite direction to me. I don't suppose you could walk me home?'

'Of course, it would be an honour,' said Tomas, allowing his French accent to surface a little more than usual. His English was excellent, almost native; he had an easy knack with languages. He had noticed, however, that Miriam was interested in anything that she saw as different or exotic.

They walked the short distance to her home in silence. At the door, she stood for a moment, unsure. 'Tomas, would you like to go somewhere with me? This weekend?'

'I'd love to,' he said, then fell quiet. He was so scared of saying or doing the wrong thing that he was struck dumb.

She smiled. 'You're very good-looking. I suppose you've had lots of girlfriends.'

He paused, surprised by her blunt honesty, considering the implications of any answer he could possibly make, and she giggled. 'I won't give you the third degree. Pick me up after lunch tomorrow? We'll go for a walk.'

Tomas smiled, relieved. He looked at her, wondering if he should kiss her. She looked as if she expected to be kissed, so he brushed her lips gently with his own. She closed her eyes for a moment and then turned, opening the front door and leaving him standing on the steps, happily confused.

Back at the pub, he found Anthony already in bed. When Tomas put the light on, he pushed his head out from under the covers. 'How did it go?' he asked sleepily.

'Wonderful,' sighed Tomas. 'How about you?'

'Oh, she's nice enough.' Anthony screwed his eyes up against the light, and retreated back under the blankets. Tomas lay awake for a long time, enjoying the familiar warmth and smell of his twin next to him, thinking of the smile on the face of the woman he was falling in love with.

Time passed, and it felt like they'd always been in Bardale, part of village life. Tomas and Miriam were a popular couple, and the three of them were often seen together.   The crowd in the village hall were noisy and, as Tomas led them in a singalong, Anthony took the opportunity to slip out into the warm, late summer night. The hall had been thick with cigarette smoke, and the young man felt suffocated. He looked up at the sky. The stars were thick in the velvet black, and he moved away from the yellow glow of the windows to let his eyes adjust to the darkness. He walked behind the hall, it was darker there, and he leaned against the wall. Looking at the stars he suddenly realised he was wrenchingly homesick for his family, his home. He could hear Tomas inside, bringing rock and roll to the English countryside. He smiled wryly, and wondered if he'd be able to persuade his twin to leave Miriam alone for long enough to go for a long walk that night. He had to find some way to release his pent up energy, and a hill walk might help.

A movement caught his eye, and Miriam peered around the side of the building. She giggled, and moved over to him, pushing her long dark curls back from her eyes. She tripped, and looked at him wide-eyed.

'Tom? Fancy a quickie? We've got time, your Tony's keeping everyone occupied in there.'

Anthony winced. He loathed being called 'Tony'. And he knew that Miriam knew that. The woman was closer now, leaning in to him. There wasn't nearly enough alcohol on her breath to account for her behaviour, and he couldn't detect any sign of dope either. He watched her, warily.

'Tom, baby. We can go under the bridge. Do you want to do it under the bridge?'

'I'm not Tomas,' he said evenly, refusing to move away from her.

She was pressing against him, reaching up to pull his earlobe. 'Funny guy. Who are you then? Anthony?'

'Yeah, I'm Anthony. You know that perfectly well.' He closed his eyes. 'What's this about?'

Abruptly, the weight against his chest disappeared, as Miriam stood straight. She shrugged. 'It's odd, the two of you. So alike in some ways. I just wondered, how alike are you?'

She flashed a quick, nervous smile. 'Tom's got secrets...'

'Has he?'

'I thought, you know, you might be less ... secretive.'

'You were after pillow talk? That's what they call it, right?' He shook his head. 'Forget it, Miriam. If Tomas has secrets, they're his to keep. I bet you have a few of your own.'

'Me? I'm an open book. It's you two. Turning up, out of the blue, never talking about the past, about your family...'

'We're orphans. Been alone since we were fourteen.'

She frowned. 'Tom said that. But surely there

are cousins, aunts, uncles?'

'Just us,' Anthony said quietly. 'We've travelled Europe together since we were just fourteen. We looked older than that, managed to get work. We stuck together. That's why we're here … looking for family, really.'

'Have you found any?'

'Not yet.' The young man managed a smile. 'Look, don't worry about Tom. He thinks the world of you. Just go with the flow, eh? Oh, and stop trying to seduce other men, you're just not that good at it.'

She turned to go, then stopped, her back to him. 'Anthony…'

'Yeah?'

'Don't tell him.'

'I wouldn't dream of it.'

Chapter 4

The sun had taken its time going down, but when darkness finally came, the depth of it almost took Eddie by surprise. He'd been dozing in the kitchen chair, his mug of tea had gone cold, and the back door stood open, as he'd left it.

He shook his head; it was a daft thing to do, with Frannie fast asleep upstairs. The farm road was a long one, and any stranger would probably set off the chickens, or the dog, or the cows, but it wasn't like Eddie to doze off. He checked that the chicken house was fastened shut, took a final stroll around the farmyard, then locked up and made his way upstairs. Frannie's door was ajar, and he peered in, seeing her asleep, curled on her side. She was so pale, so fragile. He bit his lip and went to his own room, shutting the curtains and taking a thick leather file out of the drawer. He browsed through old letters, and thick sheets of paper, some new, some ancient, bound with ribbons. Loosening one of the ribbons, he selected a document and settled down to read it. It was in his own hand, written twenty years ago, transcribed from notes made from a conversation with his grandfather.

> They lived among us. People have forgotten about them. There were four or five families, but they intermarried with each other, and with us. You should remember that: their blood is still in us, in the village, in the farms. They were powerful people, strong and hard-

working, and given to odd talents. They were a fertile folk, so I heard; children every year, and those kids didn't die when the measles or the chicken pox came round. Oh, they were as helpless as anyone when it came to accidents, but if an illness swept through, those people might lose a baby or two, but most of the family was left standing. You notice things like that, or my grandma noticed, and told me, and I'm telling you.

I'm saying you should watch out for them, because you need to know about them if they come back. You need to know what they can do. I'm not saying they're bad, or dangerous, although there's no reason they can't be. I am saying it's better if you know.

They don't need sleep like we do. Not the adults, anyway; the children need as much sleep as ours do. The grown men and women will work and play all day and all night, then maybe on the second or third night they'll need a few hours. Doesn't mean they can't sleep, if there's nothing better to do, they'll settle to it as easy as you or I do. It gives them an advantage, in business, in life – four or five hours a day awake when everyone else is asleep. Think what you could do with that.

They don't get ill, or if they do, they're well the next day. That's something to watch out for. They heal fast: scratch their arm and there's no sign the next day. If they break a limb, they're right as rain within a week or two.

They usually have a trade, and they're usually very good at it, men and women both. Of course, they have the time to learn, but they apply themselves too, they're not easily distracted. They start a job, and they finish it, and they get pleasure from finishing it.

This is an odd one – one that my grandma told me, and one they try to hide: they always have twin babies. My grandma swore that every birth, there's someone from the families goes away the next day, usually a woman and a man. I've been told that they take one of the twins for fostering, somewhere far away. It makes sense, because those big families, they always have room for foster babies that come in from outside. I guess they're the spare twins from other families, far away. I don't know why they don't raise them as twins, maybe they draw too much attention, I don't know.

This is the thing, the thing you won't believe: these people can change their shape. They are wolf people. This is a true thing. Don't listen to the fairy stories, or the old wives' tales, listen to me. There were people living in this valley, in these hills, who could be walking like you or I one minute, then the next could be running like a wolf – a big wolf – without a care in the world. They did it because they could. They'd hunt, they'd pick out an old or injured animal and put it down quietly and cleanly. They ran around in the hills for fun, because they enjoyed it. They never hurt a soul, remember that – not one person.

And they married out, some of them. They were as likely to fall in love with someone out of their five families as in them, and they made good husbands and wives. The few children that came from those marriages were weak, and there were never many grandchildren, but love doesn't care, and the werewolves, because that's what I'll call them, the werewolves were strong and they worked hard, and they made money enough to take care of their weaker children and grandchildren, the ones who weren't like them, and weren't quite like us either.

They're gone now, and another day I'll tell you about that, because I'm tired now, and it's a story that takes some strength to tell. But remember what to look for. Strong people, who don't need a lot of sleep. Twins, maybe, if they're not being too cautious. They'll be back, because they love this part of the world. Watch out for them.

Eddie stacked the sheets again, and retied the ribbon. He murmured to himself. 'Watch out for them, Grandad? What did you mean? Be wary of them? Or take care of them? I should have asked.'

Anthony pushed his hair back. It was damp with

sweat. The sun was hot on his bare shoulders, and if he closed his eyes he was back home, the heat was sheer pleasure. He was repairing a wall in Eddie's top field. The job was nearly done, and he was looking forward to getting back to the farmhouse for a cold drink. He checked his watch. Two thirty – still time to finish the job, get back to the pub, have a wash, and maybe see if Linda fancied some company. Tomas was labouring on a building site near Lancaster and wouldn't be back until after six.

He chinked the wall, fitting small stones into the gaps, and stood back, looking at his work. Not impressive, but looked after properly it would stay solid for a century, at least. He was satisfied, and pulled on his shirt. It was a ten-minute walk to the farmhouse and when he arrived Eddie was sitting in the kitchen, nursing a cup of tea and reading the *Daily Mirror*.

'Can I come in?' Anthony asked politely, standing in the doorway.

'Aye, lad. Don't stand about. Tea?' the farmer raised his mug.

'I'll have some water, if you don't mind?'

'Aye, it's in t'tap.' Eddie waved at the sink, and Anthony picked up a pint mug from the draining board and filled it with cold water. He sipped at it at first, then drained the mug, refilling it and drinking back another pint.

'Hot out there? I thowt tha'd be used to it, being from abroad.' Eddie was direct.

'I like it, it reminds me of home. Do you need me for any more jobs today, Mr Shepherd?'

'Nay. It's too nice to work. Frannie can milk t'cows when she gets back. Shall I see you in t'Dog tonight?'

'I don't know. I was going to ask Linda out. What do you think?'

Eddie surveyed him critically. 'How long have you two been courting.'

Anthony privately thought that 'courting' was too strong a word, but he humoured the man.

'A month, maybe six weeks.'

'Aye, she's a fine girl. Good stock too. She got a prize, you know?'

Anthony's mind was in overdrive. He had a mental image of Linda being led around a stock pen, a large red rosette pinned to her prim little schoolteacher's suit.

'A prize?' he managed at last.

'Aye, good stock. Pretty too, I suppose.' Eddie offered no further information.

'Well, I like her,' managed Anthony.

Eddie squinted at him. 'You're not meeting her like that?'

The young man shook his head. 'No, I'm going back to the Dog. I'll have a quick wash and get changed.'

Eddie smiled. It was a rare event, and made him look closer to thirty than forty. 'Nay, you've worked hard today. I've got more hot water than I can use. Treat yourself to a bath. Mind you clean it out though after, or you'll have Frannie to deal with.'

'Well, I don't want to get on the wrong side of Frannie,' joked Anthony. He had a healthy respect for the sharp tongue of his employer's young daughter.

'It's upstairs. It's a proper bathroom. Wife made me have it put in. Have it as deep as you like. Use my razor if you want. You want to look nice to court Linda.'

The young man was touched. 'Thank you, Eddie. I appreciate it.'

He ran a hot bath, and sank into it. He was shocked and disgusted to see the grime that rose from his skin. The shower at the pub provided a listless dribble at best, and a daily top and tail wash at the basin was clearly not enough. He suddenly realised that Eddie may have had his own comfort in mind, as well as Anthony's. He smiled ruefully, realising that his boss had been subtly telling him to get rid of the smell. When he got back, he would have to have a word with Tomas.

He scrubbed enthusiastically, starting to sing. It was amazing how happy a tub of hot water suddenly made him. Finished, he jumped out and dried himself on a threadbare hand towel, enjoying the cold lino of the bathroom. He shaved carefully, and picked up his clothes. He was clean, but he realised that his clothes were not. He decided to change into his other set at the pub, and spend some of his wages on buying new clothes. He dressed, combed his hair back, and wiped the tub carefully, making sure that he dried it and left the taps sparkling. Eddie was right – the wrath of Frannie was a terrifying thing. She was only sixteen, three long years younger than him, but she had a knack of making him feel like a naughty child if he left anything untidy in 'her' kitchen. She had a couple of jobs, in the kitchen at the White Bull at lunchtimes, and waitressing in a cafe in the nearest town on Saturdays.

He walked back to the pub, to the room he shared with his twin. He changed his clothes and took the dirty ones downstairs. The landlady was in the small laundry room. 'About time too,' she commented drily, pointing to a painted wicker basket. 'Pop them in there.'

Anthony smiled his thanks, and made his way to the bar. He was picking up the receiver on the phone when the door opened. Linda stuck her head into the bar and looked round. When she saw Anthony she smiled broadly.

'I was looking for you,' she said.

'I was ringing you,' he replied.

They stood and looked at each other. Then he went over to the door and escorted her outside. 'And why were you ringing me?' she asked.

Anthony put his arm around her shoulders. 'I was going to ask if you wanted to come looking for me.'

'Cheeky boy. It's a nice day. I didn't want to sit indoors marking books. Would you like to walk with me? By the river?'

'I've the rest of the day free, so that sounds good.'

They walked close together, but not holding hands. As they turned away from the village and out of sight of the road, Linda took a quick look round and raised her face slightly, closing her eyes. Anthony took his cue and kissed her, lightly. She opened her mouth slightly and he responded, pulling her closer. Things were going slowly with this woman, who might one day be his wife, but he was oddly disinclined to move things along. Tomas's raucous tales of Miriam's behaviour was giving Anthony a new appreciation for the quiet reserve of the woman he was courting. The thought of Miriam aroused him though, and he thought back to the previous night. A shocked gasp brought him back to the present. He realised that he'd slipped his hand beneath Linda's blouse, working it free of her skirt. He was caressing her breast through the heavy lace of her bra, gently thumbing her nipple, which was amazingly hard.

'Anthony, no.' She was as still as a trapped bird, he could feel her heart beating fast.

'Hell, I'm sorry.' He moved his hand away, every nerve in it remembering the feel of her breast under his fingers, the astounding hardness and heat of that nipple. She was breathing hard, and he could smell her arousal. His body was responding fast, and he knew that with one lie he could have this woman. If he told her that he loved her, she would fall into his hands like an apple from the tree.

He drew away and watched as she tucked her blouse back into her skirt. She was blushing hard now. Eventually she looked up. 'I'm sorry, Anthony, that was my fault as much as yours. Shall we carry on?'

He was dizzily confused, and then he realised

she was referring to the walk. 'Oh, yes. Linda, I'm sorry too.'

They continued, Linda eventually starting to chat again, telling him stories about the children in her class. Eventually, the subject came around to the annual country show, and how some of the farm children were busy preparing their chickens and ducks for the poultry show. Anthony laughed. 'That reminds me. Eddie told me you won a prize when you were young. The way he said it made you sound like a prize heifer!'

'I bet Eddie said I was from good stock too?' She was smiling.

'He did!' Anthony was relieved, the awkwardness had gone.

'I've known Eddie since I was a little girl. I'm a distant cousin of his wife, you know? Well, he's partly right. You know my mum died young?'

'I did, actually. It's a small village, and people talk.'

'She'd got pregnant again when I was about nine. Something went wrong, and we lost her and the baby. Dad brought me up. But he'll live until he's a hundred.'

Anthony nodded. He was almost certain that Linda's mother had been a half-blood; there was a fifty per cent chance that Linda was too. He felt vaguely ashamed of himself.

She continued, smiling. 'Well, I got a prize when I left school. Not a day missed. Nursery, infants, primary, secondary, sixth form. I was the same at teacher training college, except for a couple

Fight for the Future

of sick days because of a hangover. I'm like dad,' she said proudly.

'Are you?' said Anthony. He felt a crushing disappointment, but couldn't bring himself to regret the last few weeks. Linda was a sweet woman.

'What's wrong?' she asked him, picking up on his sudden change in mood.

'Nothing.'

'Is it because of before, because...'

His hand was suddenly alive with memory, and he could feel her curves beneath his palm. He scratched his palm with his fingernails, and the sensation was gone.

'No, really. It's not. It's not important.'

He spoke absently. He'd lost any physical enthusiasm he had for the woman. He was wondering how he was going to extricate himself from the relationship without losing her friendship, which he had come to genuinely value.

Linda was silent for a while, then spoke tentatively. 'Anthony?'

'Yes?'

'Can I ask you something?'

'Of course.'

'Well, we've been seeing each other for a few weeks. I know it's not long, but I was wondering how you saw things going?'

He looked up, alert.

'Going? Well, I'd not really looked that far ahead. I thought we were just having fun. I enjoy your company, you're funny and you're nice to look at.' He recovered himself. 'Beautiful to look at,' he added.

Linda gave a small, shaky laugh. 'Funny and nice to look at. Thanks, Anthony. At least I'm not "nice, and funny to look at". The trouble is, I'm getting in too deep. I know myself, I've been here before. And honestly, I'm getting too old to waste any more time on something that won't work out.'

Anthony gave her a questioning look.

She continued, not looking at him. 'I think I might be falling in love with you. Which would be stupid. You're a lot younger than me. I know you are. It's the things you say. You look older ... but you're not ready to settle down, are you? Anyway, you might not even be here in six months. You could be in Italy, or France, or America. Will you go? When Tomas and Miriam get married? Or were you going to stay?'

He shrugged. 'I've no plans. Don't fall in love with me, Linda. I don't think it would do either of us any good.'

She looked away quickly. When she looked back her face was composed, but her eyes gleamed suspiciously.

'I thought it was like that for you, but I had to make sure. I'm sorry. Maybe it's best if we break it off now.'

'If that's how you want it.' He managed to convey deep disappointment. 'I'm sorry, Linda, I do like you, but not enough for what you want. I'll walk you home. Would that be OK?'

She nodded. They turned back, and walked silently to the small house that she shared with her father. He kissed her forehead, and gave her a quick hug. There didn't seem to be anything to say, so he didn't say it. Within minutes he was back at the pub. He locked the door, drew the curtains, lay down, and thought things through. He spread out on the double bed, enjoying having it to himself. It was about time he and Tomas found better accommodation; they'd been in the village for a while now.

Maybe it was time to move away, to leave Tomas to his new life. He mentally checked through the list of female possible half-bloods that he'd drawn up, using village gossip and information from his own mother about her grandmother's family.

Miriam was Tomas's fiancée now. They were actually making wedding plans, much to the chagrin of Jennison, her ex-fiancé. Linda had seemed like a likely candidate, her mother almost certainly had suffered the sickness that came with the half-blood. But no half-blood could ever be so disgustingly healthy as the schoolteacher. Her mother had died without passing the trait on. Another potential, Ellie Hetherington, was married, forty, and had one sickly teenaged son. Anthony was as convinced as he could be that they were both half-blood, but it made no difference to his situation. Dammit. He'd wanted to find someone local, and stay with Tomas. They could protect each other from danger – local or from abroad. He sighed. The only other potential candidate left was Ingrid, the sloppy thirty-something assistant at the bakery in the next village. She was married, irritating, and dull. He shuddered. He'd rather die childless.

Jeanette Greaves

The family history charts that he'd drawn up had four other names. Three little girls, ranging from three to eight years old, and Eddie's wife's sister, who had been dead for fifteen years. Eddie's wife had definitely not been marked by the half-blood sickness. She had died only a year ago, a typically stupid farm accident. She'd been kicked in the head by a horse that she was helping to geld at the next farm. Eddie talked about her a lot, and it was clear that she'd been a healthy vibrant woman who he'd loved dearly. Frances's six younger sisters were still being fostered by relatives while Eddie got over his grief. Frannie had stayed at home to look after her father. With seven children, there was no way that Eddie or his dead wife had carried the trait. Maybe it *was* time to move away, maybe go to Italy, follow up the rumours there. He'd hang around, wait until Tomas was safely married, then leave.

His thoughts slipped back to Linda, the way she'd felt in his arms. He sat up, suddenly determined. He could think of better things to spend his money on than clothes. He opened his guitar case and took out the money he'd managed to save. He scrawled a note for Tomas, asking him to tell Eddie that he'd be away for a day or two, and ran downstairs, just managing to get on the last bus out of the village.

He was the only person on the bus. The conductor lit a cigarette and came and sat next to him. 'You're one of them foreign twins,' he observed.

'I'm one of them,' the young man confirmed.

'The one who pinched Miriam Hartnell from

the Jennison lad?'

'No, the other one.' Anthony found himself in good humour.

'Ah then, t'other one. You'll be courting t'teacher then?'

Anthony fought the temptation to roll his eyes. The men in Lancashire could gossip better than the women, and that was saying something.

'I'm not, no. She broke things off today.' There – that would make her happy, and keep the gossips busy.

'Sorry, lad. I thowt she would. Her old dad doesn't like dagos. So you're off to drown your sorrows?'

'Yes. Any recommendations?'

The conductor smiled at him. He was a fat little man, with hair springing from his ears. He favoured Anthony with a 'both men of the world' expression. 'The Dog and Duck in town'd be the place to start. Watch out for the women in there, though, they're not all as good as they should be.'

'I'll watch out very carefully. Thanks.'

The conductor winked, and made his way down the bus back to the driver, regaling him with the new Bardale gossip.

'Dog and Duck it is then,' muttered Anthony to himself, watching the landscape crawl past.

Chapter 5

Three days later he woke up on a bench in Liverpool. The noise of the ships and the din from the docks was phenomenal. He groaned. He'd left the village determined to get drunk and get laid, and his body was telling him that he'd succeeded very well. He'd also been robbed. Again. He found a fence and started to pee against it, the sudden agony in his belly a testament to the weekend. He'd caught something nasty. Again.

'Bloody women,' he whispered, watching a few drops of dark piss fall to the ground. There was nothing else for it. He felt a sudden ache of longing: homesickness. He closed his eyes, seeing darkly green hillsides, a fast, shallow river on a bed of jutting rocks, a smoky pub, the tang of the trees outside his bedroom window. Bardale. He had to get back.

He made his way on foot out of the city. It took him an hour to find his way to the nearest suburbs, gardens – and cover. He shed his filthy clothes and dropped to all fours. It had been months since he'd allowed himself this release, the pleasure of changing. He got his bearings, buried his clothes, and headed north.

As the day passed, as the sun got higher in the sky, life became simpler. His wolf mind became more dominant, taking a simple pleasure in the heat of the sun, the chill of the air from the sea. He skirted villages, towns, farms, making a steady pace back towards where he knew his twin was waiting. He paused to drink from a river, drawing back in disgust

Fight for the Future

at the stink of chemicals and the oily sheen on the water. He detoured uphill, finding a pure stream and drinking his fill. He ignored the sheep dotted on the hillside; he wasn't hungry, and he knew not to touch livestock. He zig-zagged back down the hill, keeping low, invisible.

In the heat of early afternoon, he found shade in an old barn. He turned around in the ancient hay, finding comfort in ritual. When he awoke, he was naked and human. He needed to piss again, and did so against the outside of the barn. This time it was clean and painless. He sighed with relief; the infection hadn't survived the sudden change of form of the host body. Sometimes it did, and he had to change three or four times until he beat an infection. He had a vague understanding that if he could only teach himself to change faster, more cleanly, he could beat sickness every time.

He peered out of the barn. It was early evening. He could see a road, half a mile away. He looked round quickly, and decided to risk it. He walked through the hayfield, unbothered by his nakedness, and vaulted over the drystone wall. Just on the other side, a road sign told him where he was, and how far he had to travel. He was satisfied – his wolf instincts had been sending him in the right direction. He climbed the wall again, and bent for the change. Alone, he felt more confident about experimentation. When Tomas was around he always felt that tradition was expected of him.

He deliberately slowed the change, trying to understand what was happening. It was the will, he knew that. He had to *will* himself to be a different shape. Sometimes, if his will was weak, if he felt safe enough, he would change back to his human shape in his sleep, or if his concentration lapsed. He suspected that there were many things about his body that he didn't know or understand, but he was happy to settle for this glorious trick, this wild release. The downside, of course, was this overwhelming, constant need to know that he'd passed on the trait. In the absence of a true mate, he had to find a half-blood, and hope for a child to carry on his line.

He experimented for a while, in the cover of the wall, trying to see how slowly and how fast he could change from human to wolf, and back again. The faster he did it, the more painless it seemed to be. Changing back to human was the easier way. He could do it in his sleep, he reflected wryly.

All the changing had made him hungry, so he hunted for a while in the twilight. A couple of fat rabbits and half a dozen field mice filled him nicely. He found clean running water leaking from a pipe leading to a farmhouse. It was treated water, chlorinated, but he drank it happily, his tail wagging. Fed, watered and rested, he set off back to Bardale at a steady trot.

It was early on Monday morning when he got back to the village. People were already up and about, and he slunk around to the pub, hopefully nosing at the back door. It was shut fast. He glanced up at his bedroom window. It was open a little, but not enough for him to scramble through. He considered the consequences of being seen climbing the walls of the pub naked, and looked for another solution. Howling or attempting to bark was out of the question. Keeping to his wolf shape, he turned and marked his scent on the wall directly under the bedroom window. He whined, as quietly as he could. He waited.

A couple of minutes later his twin leaned out of the window, wrinkling his nose. 'Where on earth have you been? Hang on, I'll open the door.'

Anthony waited, and Tomas soon appeared at the back door. The wanderer followed his twin inside and up the stairs, letting him hold the bedroom door open. He changed back to human form.

Tomas looked at him. 'You've got about an hour before Mrs Martin makes you get up.'

'I know.'

'Where've you been? I was getting worried.'

'Lancaster and Liverpool, that much I'm sure of. Maybe other places too. I'm sure it was fun.'

Tomas sat on the edge of the bed. 'Tell me.'

'I would if I could bloody well remember anything. I think I got an invitation to a party in Lancaster. And I have vague memories of playing someone else's guitar at a party somewhere. It doesn't matter, I'm home now.'

Tomas nodded. 'Eddie grunted when I told him you'd gone AWOL. You'd better find him today if you want to keep your job.'

Anthony frowned. 'Ah, yes. I'll go straight to the farm. If he thinks I've got out of bed early he'll be more inclined to forgive me. What are you doing?'

Tomas grinned with excitement. 'I've got a job. A proper job, I mean. The building work is nearly finished in Lancaster, and the plumbers are in. One of them has offered me an apprenticeship. He says I'm a bit old to be starting, but he likes me, and he says I'm strong enough to carry things around for him.'

'That's great. Just make sure he trains you up well.'

Tomas sat back on the bed and hugged his twin. 'I will. I've missed you.'

Anthony hugged him back. 'I had to get back to you too. And the village, I've missed this place. Any news?'

'Oh, I forgot. Linda has told everyone that she's going to apply for a job in Manchester. She's moving away. Why did she break things off with you?'

Anthony raised an eyebrow.

Tomas smiled. 'Oh, I see. She's not the one.'

'Not exactly like that. She's not the one, but that wasn't it. She gave me the "what are your intentions?" speech. By then I knew that she wasn't what we're looking for, so I gave her the "boys just want to have fun" speech back. She finished with me there and then.'

'So what are we going to do?' Tomas looked worried.

His brother sighed. 'Oh, I don't know. There were some male half-bloods further up the line, our parents' generation. They moved away from the village. Maybe I could try to find where they went, see if they have any daughters or granddaughters of the right age. If that doesn't work out I'll hang around until you're settled, then take it from there. Any other news?'

'Oh yes, the best. We've got a gig. A wedding in town. The girl is a huge Everly Brothers fan, and her dad came into the pub last night looking for us. He asked me if we could play that sort of stuff.'

'Better than they can, and you've got a better voice.' Anthony smiled. 'OK, have you got any money? I need clothes, and I'll nip into Lancaster next weekend and get the records. We'll borrow little Frannie's player and we can learn the songs. When's the gig?'

Tomas stared at him. 'You got robbed? Again? Another whore?'

'Well, I know what they're up to, but I can earn money a lot more easily than they can. I don't mind.'

'You don't mind when you know that I'll bail you out, you mean! The gig's in a month's time. The money is good. Twenty pounds.'

'Each?'

'Don't push your luck. I got it up from fifteen because I said we knew all the songs. It'll be a long night, and I've sorted us free drinks and a pick at the buffet too. And I said we'd dress like the Yanks too. We can buy clothes from that second-hand shop in Lancaster. Good stuff. All the best people dump their old stuff there.'

'You've done well.'

Chapter 6

The brothers parted after the usual heavy breakfast. Anthony walked to the farm. The day promised to be beautiful again. He didn't care that he was penniless, but he hoped he wasn't going to find himself jobless. He wanted to make a good impression in the village, and he suspected that he may have fouled things up.

In the lane, he passed Frannie on her bicycle. She stopped and regarded him through cynical dark-brown eyes. 'You came back,' she observed. It wasn't a question. He couldn't think of a reply; he felt completely chastened.

'Well, there's work to be done. Dad's upset. Barney died last night. Be nice to him when you get there.' She favoured him with one more contemptuous glance, then rode towards town. He stood and watched for a while. Her straight black hair was tied back in pigtails, and he wondered if she knew that her schoolgirl hairstyle was completely at odds with her adult demeanour. He suspected that if she did know, she didn't care.

At the farmhouse, he found Eddie desultorily chewing on cold toast. A small bundle, wrapped in an old pillowcase, lay by the empty fireplace. The farmer looked up when Anthony knocked on the open door.

'Come in, lad. How many times have I told you not to knock?'

'Frannie tells me I have to knock.'

'Ah well, it's my farm. Just come in. Unless she's around of course, then you'd better knock.'

The two men exchanged a complicit smile.

Anthony nodded at the bundle. 'Old Barney? I'm sorry.'

The terrier had been officially employed on the farm as a rat-catcher, but it was no secret that he was a much-loved pet too. He must have been eleven or twelve years old, and hadn't caught so much as a baby mouse in the last few months. The mice and rats were getting out of control. Eddie refused to use poison, claiming that it was cruel to put even a rat through that sort of agony.

Anthony had seen two or three small, young rats laid out on the kitchen step a few weeks earlier. A young roaming tomcat had found the farm, and was clearly trying to make a home there. Frannie had fed the cat, giving it some encouragement, and had been rewarded with a neat row of mice almost every morning since. His ratting ability was clearly not up to the job though. Now that Barney was dead, Eddie would be looking for a pup.

The man looked up, his pale-blue eyes dry but red-rimmed. 'Aye. He were a good dog. I'll find another terrier though. I hear there's a Jack Russell bitch expecting a mongrel litter over near Carnforth way. The sire's a terrier too, although that's as specific as anyone'd dared to get wi' it. I know the dog, he's a damn good ratter himself.'

He grinned. 'Mebbe I'll have a couple of the pups. What do you think?'

'It's nice to have a brother around,' answered Anthony. 'What does the bitch's owner think?'

'She's spitting blood. She was planning to

breed the bitch to a Jack Russell stud, make some money from selling the pups. Instead, she'll have a litter of mongrel terriers that she'll have trouble getting rid of. Mongrels are ten a penny.'

'Good ratters are valuable though. You'll miss Barney.'

'Aye. Think I'll take a trip over to Carnforth today, introduce meself, ask her to keep two or three of the litter. If she's not got homes promised, she might get rid of the whole litter. I don't want that, not if they're fine pups. I had Barney's sister too, you know. Had her fixed so she didn't have pups. We never had time for that, too many kids in the house to have time for pups too.'

He looked around at the empty kitchen. 'Mebbe it's time for me to get my girls back. I reckon I can deal with 'em now.'

Anthony nodded. 'Will you still need me? When your daughters come home?'

Eddie looked up, surprised. 'Of course. They're nowt but kids. Frannie will whip them into shape, but they're too young to do any heavy work.' He glanced at the bundle again. 'I'll send word out to them to come home next week, give Frannie a chance to air their rooms out. Come on, lad. Let's get this dog buried.'

The two men dug a deep grave for the little dog, safe from foxes, under a tree in the back garden. Eddie wiped his face as they finished, and Anthony pretended it was just sweat that the man was wiping away from his eyes.

They went back to the kitchen, and Eddie

made a pot of tea. 'We'll have a bit of a sit down, then there's work to do. I won't ask where tha's bin.'

'Sorry about that. I just had to run a bit mad. Linda finished with me...'

'Aye, I heard. And you went running off to find a more open-minded sort of woman. From the look of you, you found one. I'm not daft.'

The farmer paused. 'I sometimes wonder if I should marry again. I'm not forty yet. But mebbe I'm cursed.'

'Cursed?' Anthony looked up, curious.

'Aye. Losing one wife is bad enough, losing two is a bit careless.'

'Two?' The farmhand was surprised.

'Aye. Didn't you know? Lily was my second wife. She was always the one I loved, always, but we had a misunderstanding when we were young, and I started seeing her sister, to make her jealous. Daftest thing I ever did, because poor little Dottie got caught. I had to marry her, straight off. My Frances is Dottie's lass through and through. Poor Dottie didn't last long after Frances was born, never got over it. Lily and I waited a year or so before we got wed. For the sake of appearances, she said. If I could live my life over, I would have left Dottie well alone. Lily always told me it wasn't my fault, her sister would have died young anyway, she was always a sickly sort. But I was out of order anyway. The woman deserved better than a husband with a hankering for someone else.'

Eddie stared at the table. 'We do awful things when we're young, us men. Then we have daughters,

Jeanette Greaves

and I guess watching and worrying about them is our punishment. Still, mine are still just girls. Alreet, Anthony? You've gone a funny colour.'

'Sorry, Eddie, just the weekend catching up with me.' Anthony was stunned. Frannie? First of all, he thought of her as a kid. Secondly, she might not have the half-blood, despite the new knowledge he had of her parentage. He realised that curiosity wouldn't be out of place.

'Does Frances know that Lily wasn't her mother?'

'Oh yes, but nobody really bothers about it. They were close, those two. Lily always said that Frances had been here before. She's always been too old for her years. She knows too much.'

Anthony shifted uncomfortably. 'I get that feeling too.'

'Aye lad, she's got you sussed.' Eddie's eyes were sparkling.

'Really?'

'Oh aye. The first time she met you she told me you'd work hard, but I wasn't to rely on you.'

Anthony blushed deep red. 'I'm sorry. You can rely on me now. I just had to...'

'Get it out of your system. I know.' Eddie fell silent, considering. 'While we're talking, there's one other thing. I know you and your brother are close, but would you consider moving out of the pub and in with us? It's a bit cheeky of me.'

'Cheeky?' Anthony blinked.

'Well, I've been paying you casual, piecework, and it's getting a bit much now that you're always

Fight for the Future

here. My farmhands usually live in and get a bit of a smaller wage, but board as well. You'll be just as well off as you are now if you're not paying out for bed and breakfast at the Dog. There's a wee shed next t'barn where the farm lads usually live. When my girls are home, I'll feel better having another man around, to keep an eye on the place when I'm in town.'

He nodded to Anthony. 'I let things get out of hand when Lily died. Went a bit mad, I think. Frances kept it together, as much as she could, and I'm ashamed that I let her. The last lad I had working for me left in a strop because I wasn't in the best of moods. You can clean the shed out, there's a proper bed in there, and somewhere to keep your things.'

'Is it dry? Properly dry? I can't have damp getting to my guitar.'

'Aye, it's dry. You can spend tomorrow sorting it out, making sure it's up to your standards. I'll start paying you proper wages from today. Is it a deal?'

Anthony tried to keep his smile from becoming too broad. The arrangement suited him well. 'It's a deal. Will Frances be OK?'

'Frannie will do as she's told. And I'll sweeten the pill for her – you can do the early milking instead of her. Does that suit?'

The men shook on the deal, and spent the rest of the day working companionably.

At half past six, Anthony returned to the pub to collect his guitar. Tomas was napping on the bed.

'Leaving again?' he asked, sleepily.

'Not quite. But I'm moving to the Shepherd place. Eddie's decided to trust me enough to let me live there. I'll still be around. Do you mind?'

Tomas stretched out. 'Mind? I'll have the bed to myself. Don't forget about that wedding gig.'

'No, we'll meet up and practise.'

Tomas looked at him. 'Why are you grinning like that?'

Anthony was the picture of innocence. He'd decided to keep his discovery quiet for the time being. 'Just because life is going well. For both of us. I'll see you tomorrow night in the pub?'

'Make it Wednesday. I'm taking Miriam out tomorrow.'

'Wednesday then.'

Tomas swallowed. 'I'm going to miss you.'

Anthony looked at his twin, suddenly realising that this parting was the first real one of their lives. Always before they'd shared a room, they'd seen each other almost every day. Even separated, they'd known they would come back to each other. He reached out and hugged Tomas. 'Be careful, brother. I won't be here to watch your back.'

'I'll be fine. And Miriam will look after me.'

Anthony privately doubted Miriam's inclination to look after anyone other than herself, but decided to give her the benefit of the doubt. He picked up his guitar case and left, carrying nothing else but a change of underwear and a toothbrush.

When he got back to the farm he was tired and hungry. Eddie was doing his last rounds, checking the livestock, making sure the chickens were safe in the henhouse. 'You're staying tonight then? That's good. There's still some stew in the pot, if you want to warm it up for supper. Help yourself to bread and butter. I've told Frannie that you're moving in.'

'How did she take it?'

'She didn't seem bothered either way. She said to remind you that breakfast is at six thirty prompt though.' Eddie frowned. 'Do me a favour, if you're feeling awake. Some kid on a motorbike called round for Frances earlier. It's not Steven, the kid who she was seeing at Christmas. It's someone a bit older than her. She said she met him at the cafe. Will you stay up until she gets home? I'm tired out.'

Anthony shook his head. 'She's just a kid. What's she playing at?'

'She's sixteen. Old enough to go courting, she made that plain to me. I made sure that lad got a look at my shotgun before he rode off with her, but I'd appreciate it if you'd stay up to make sure he doesn't hang around when he brings her back.'

'I will.'

Eddie sighed loudly. 'I'm off to bed. Early start again tomorrow. I wasted last year, just kept things ticking over, but that's never good enough on a farm. I think I lost track when Lily died. There's a lot to do, repairs and stuff. Goodnight, lad.' He went to bed, leaving Anthony to finish off the stew, packing it down with lots of fresh but densely untasty bread, and fresh butter. The bread was Frannie's, and was terrible. He nipped up to the bathroom and brushed his teeth. Then he turned off the kitchen light and left the house.

Anthony made his way to the shed. It was actually a well-made little cabin by the side of the barn, with a real bed and thin mattress, an electric light with a paper shade, and a small, wardrobe with several wooden coat hangers lying at the bottom. Clean sheets and blankets were piled on the bed, together with a couple of clean but stained pillows. A note was lying on top of the bale. 'Change your bed every week. There's fresh bedding in the cupboard at the top of the stairs. Don't use the blue-and-yellow floral set, that's Dad's.'

Anthony smiled. Frannie's notes were always clipped, informative, and to the point. Her handwriting was very easy to read, rounded and neat. He folded it and tucked it into his pocket. As he bent to make the bed, a large black rat shot out from underneath it, running over his foot. It disappeared through a previously unseen gap in the wall. Anthony peered under the bed and saw a mess of fresh droppings. He was furious. Frannie must have cleaned the cabin of old droppings earlier. He found himself getting angry at the thought of it, of her lying on the floor, sweeping under the bed, only for vermin to ruin her work.

He realised that he was growling. He undressed quickly, and opened the door of the cabin, falling easily into wolf form. He made for the barn first, pushing lithely through a gap in the door, ignoring the two heavily pregnant queen barn cats who screamed at him and ran vertically up a twenty-foot stack of hay. The young tom was sleeping, and

Fight for the Future

the screams woke him up. He jumped three feet into the air, straight from sleep, and raised his hackles at the wolf, challenging him, protecting his territory. The black wolf glared at him, warning him away, and then turned and started to nose around the barn. He found the first rat within seconds. The adult rats were lazy, contemptuous of the cats. Anthony was sure that the rats killed any kittens.

He snapped down on the rat's back, killing it cleanly. He didn't pause to eat; he wasn't hungry, and it was an old creature, with bitter blood. The tomcat retreated, growling angrily. The wolf let himself go completely. He was enjoying himself, catching rats and dispatching them efficiently. He sniffed out nests, protected by screaming females. He killed the mothers, by claw or by tooth, and ate the babies, crunching down on fragile bones and enjoying the sweet young taste of them. He licked his chops and looked up to the loft. He could hear rats scuttling in the beams, and on the loft floor. The ladder to the loft was vertical, and he knew he could never climb it. He rolled on the floor and stood up in human form, still wild-eyed and determined. The tomcat screeched in terror, and the two queens almost fell back down the stacks in their panic to get away from this strange naked human who was climbing the ladder at an unnatural speed.

Once in the loft, he quickly returned to wolf form and finished his game. It had taken an hour, and the barn was silent. He could sense the occasional rustle of a frightened mouse, but he was happy to leave the smaller vermin to the cats. He was tempted to howl victoriously, but suppressed it. He knew this wasn't the time or the place to announce himself. He looked down at the barn floor, spotting a pile of half-raked hay, and leaped, making a soft landing and rolling to his feet. He pushed his way out of the barn. The yard was silent, but he could see and smell adult rats in the shadows. He stretched out. He could finish them off at his leisure. He'd let a few young ones live for a while, use them to train the terrier pups when they arrived. He was looking forward to it. Eddie might think that he was training them, but Anthony planned to teach them all his wolfish tricks. He loved puppies.

He padded around the farm, indulging himself. He'd almost forgotten how much fun it was to be his wolf-self. The village was a small place, and he and Tomas were wary about being spotted. It was different on the farm. With Eddie asleep, he could make it his own personal territory. To celebrate, he marked the barn with his scent. For another hour he prowled around the farm, careful not to scare the cattle. The ducks scuttled off the banks of the small pond and gathered in the middle, setting up a mildly worried quacking. He ignored them. He knew the rules: hunt only wildlife and rats. Don't touch the livestock, don't hurt the pets.

At the gate he paused to liberally mark the extent of his territory. It would have the benefit of keeping foxes and stray dogs well away from the farm. In mid flow, he realised that advertising his presence at the farm was a very bad idea, and stopped. He pricked up his ears at the sound of an approaching motorbike, and melted into the shadows. The noise stopped, unexpectedly, about half a mile from the gate. He listened carefully. All was quiet... Then he heard the girl's voice, raised in anger. There was a secret fear in that voice, one that she was hiding well enough to fool another human. He broke into a run, towards her, his ears back, his heart racing.

He could smell the stink of the motorbike's exhaust; the machine was still running. The girl was struggling in the arms of a tall, well-built man in his early twenties. He was smiling, cajoling. The wolf stepped out of the shadows and growled. The man was intent on his own prey, and didn't see him.

'Fran, didn't you have a good time? Just a kiss, if that's all you want. Just a kiss, eh?'

'No. I don't want to kiss you. You promised to just bring me home. You promised.'

'Look, I'm sorry about what happened in the cinema. How was I to know that you're frigid?'

'Let me go, Vinnie. I'll walk from here.' Her voice was full of controlled dignity. Only the wolf could hear her panic.

'Stupid girl. Look. If you try it, you might like it.' The man was pulling her closer.

Anthony growled again, more loudly. Frannie heard, twisted around and saw him. Her eyes widened, her body went slack with fear. He blinked and moved closer. The man still hadn't seen him. Anthony doubted he was seeing anything beyond the fear in Frannie's dark eyes.

'Fran, Fran. Just relax, that's right, don't fight

me.' Vinnie's voice was hoarse with appetite, his hands were at her jacket, opening the buttons hungrily. The wolf's jaws opened, he showed his teeth, dripped saliva. The rat blood on his muzzle was dark, and still glistening. His eyes took the moonlight and turned it into bright hate. Frances looked at her attacker. She was trapped between two predators, and only one of them was aware of the other. She looked once more into the yellow eyes of the wolf, and then summoned her strength, pushing at Vinnie. He was taken by surprise at the sudden resistance, and fell back. Frannie ran towards the farm, kicking off the high-heeled shoes she'd been crippled by, and making amazing time along the lane. The wolf watched admiringly for a moment, and then turned back to Vinnie. The man was cursing, picking up his gloves and moving back to the bike.

'Stupid bloody waitresses,' he was muttering.

The wolf couldn't believe he still hadn't been seen. For a moment he considered discretion, but then decided that Vinnie deserved a scare. He took another step towards him, this time growling deep and long. The man stopped dead, and turned around, facing the wolf.

'Oh Jesus,' he said. His bladder released a dark stain that spread over the front of his jeans. His legs gave way and he fell into the verge. Anthony stalked towards him, stiff-legged. He pushed his muzzle into the man's face, letting him smell the rat blood, the wildness, before leaping and twisting in an almost comic display of strength and agility. Vinnie was close to fainting with fear. He half lay on the ground, his elbow in a cowpat, as the wolf threatened him once again, and then turned and stalked into the fields, where he watched, hidden, as Vinnie staggered to his bike and took off. The bike veered and almost fell a couple of times.

Anthony raced back to the farm, leaping the fence in a sweet fluid movement, taking a short cut across the fields, diving into his cabin, becoming human again, and pulling on his trousers and shirt. He started to walk down the drive to the gate. He heard the gate clang shut and, within a minute, the girl came into sight. She looked shaken but unhurt. She jumped when she saw him, then relaxed. He waited for her, and stayed silent as he walked her back to the house, waiting for her to speak. When she did, there was a quaver in her voice.

'You moved in tonight then? I wasn't really expecting you until tomorrow.'

'Then it was good of you to get the cabin ready tonight. Thank you. Your dad asked me to wait up for you. Where's your boyfriend?'

'I don't have a boyfriend. I won't be seeing that moron again, that's certain.'

Anthony was solicitous. 'Did he try anything? Do you want me to sort him out?'

Fran turned to him, disbelieving. 'Men! It's all fighting and fu...' She trailed off, embarrassed. 'No, I can handle myself, thank you.'

'Then why are you trembling?' Anthony was pushing his luck with her, and knew it.

'I'm not trembling,' she said. Then she looked at him. 'OK, maybe I am. I thought I saw a wolf.'

Anthony laughed. 'This is Lancashire. There've been no wolves here for hundreds of years. It must have been a big dog.'

She nodded, her common sense taking over. 'Yes, possibly, an Alsatian cross, maybe. I could have been mistaken.'

'Was it safe? Did it attack you? Shall I check the stock?'

'I don't know. He seemed upset about something though. I've never run so fast in my life.'

Anthony nodded, remembering. 'Still, I'd better have a look round. It might be rabid. Are you sure you're OK?'

She looked at him. 'That ... dog. I left Vinnie alone with it. Do you think he'll be safe?'

'Do you care?' asked Anthony, genuinely interested.

She smiled. There was violence in that smile, in the tightness of her mouth, and Anthony found it exciting. He fought the feeling down.

'No, I hope it bites him. I hope it bites his ... bits off.'

He turned away, hiding his amusement. Her delicate language was a delicious contrast to her viciousness.

'Lock the doors when you go in. I'll make sure the dog has gone. And if Vinnie's still around, I'll sort him out.'

Fran looked at him. She was coolly assessing his strength. She'd seen him working on the farm for weeks, but he was a good five inches shorter than

Vinnie, and maybe forty pounds lighter.

'Leave Vinnie be. He's not worth it,' she advised.

They'd reached the house, and she let herself in, nodding her thanks to Anthony, and locking the door securely behind her. He smiled. He'd made his decision, and he realised it didn't seem to matter about the odds. Half-blood or not, he'd found his woman. Now all he had to do was convince her to take him seriously. He winced, remembering every look she'd given him over the past few weeks, most of them conveying the fact that she thought he was nothing but a gypsy, good for nothing but a few months' farm work, before he moved on. He made for the gate. He knew, absolutely, that she would watch from her window to make sure that he kept his promise to look for the dog, and to check that Vinnie had gone. It was time to start convincing her that he could be relied on. He would start by retrieving those pretty shoes from the lane.

Chapter 7

'Eddie, can I have tomorrow afternoon off? I need to go shopping, get some clothes. I'll work Sunday morning instead.' Anthony brushed his sweat-drenched hair back. He could feel that the weather was going to break, and not a day too soon – the earth was drying out.

'You young heathen. Don't you think you should be in chapel on Sunday morning?'

Anthony looked up, anxious, but the farmer was joking.

'Nay, don't worry. I'll be at chapel myself, Frannie insists on it. I'll be bringing my girls home too, after chapel. You can see the lot of 'em together. They're a damned handful, but I want 'em home again.'

'I'm sure.' Anthony smiled happily. 'It'll be nice to be around kids.'

'Well, you'll be joining us for Sunday lunch, won't you?'

'That would be great. Are you sure?' Anthony's face brightened with pleasure.

'Aye. Now, let's finish this ditch, and then I'll give you your wage. Just five pounds this week, it's a short week. Next week I'll pay you six and ten.' He stopped, Anthony was hesitating.

'Eddie, will you do me a favour? You've got a bank account?'

'Yes. I'm in business, I have to have.'

'Will you be guarantor for me? I want to open an account, start making some savings. I'm not twenty-one until next spring … does it matter?'

Eddie smiled broadly. 'You'll be reet. Savings now? This from the lad with one shirt to his name. Nay, don't blush. I know, it's not easy when you start out. Is it your brother settling down that's made you think on?'

'Something like that.'

Eddie looked at the sky. 'It's too late for today. Bank'll be shut. I'll run you into town on Monday.' He thought for a minute. 'Of course, if you're serious about this, you could open a building society account too.'

'What's that? What's the difference?'

'Well, it's harder to get the money out at short notice. It's better though, if you're thinking of settling down. It'll help you buy your own house too. You're not a local lad, you'll never get one of those council cottages, you know.'

Anthony leaned against his spade. 'Sounds ideal. We'll do that then. You go back, you look tired. I'll finish digging this ditch out. It shouldn't take more than ten minutes now.'

Eddie clapped him on the back and returned to the farmhouse. Frannie was busy cleaning out a couple of dusty kitchen cupboards. Crockery and cutlery sparkled by the side of the sink. She was preparing for the family to be reunited.

'Frannie, the lad's staying. Cut him some slack now, I know you don't like him, but he's useful, and I don't want to have to train someone else up next year because you've driven him away.'

She turned round, frowning. 'Who says I

don't like him?'

'Well, you do a good job of hiding it if you do like 'im! Mek me a brew, eh? Then run him a bath for God's sake, he stinks like a bloody pig. Leave him one of your notes, tell him we're not short of water or towels. He'll take the hint. I think he's just shy of coming in the house, not naturally mucky.'

Although Eddie had grown up with the culture of the weekly bath – 'whether you needed it or not' – the presence of a tub in his own house, and easy hot water from an oil-fired boiler had made him a glutton for a nightly soak, and he'd instilled the habit in his children too.

Frannie finished wiping out the cupboards, and set the kettle on the hob. She looked at her father. He was only in his mid thirties, but farming was a hard life and he looked older. He'd inherited the farm when he was still in his teens, the only child of old parents, and made it work, against all odds. He seemed happy enough with the new farmhand though, and she guessed she could help out by being a little less caustic with the man. She went upstairs and started to run the bath, letting the hot and cold water mix together to give the hot, almost scalding, effect that she herself enjoyed. The sliver of soap by the side of the bath looked mean, so she took a new bar of Lux from the cabinet, unwrapping it and laying it on a dry flannel. She left him a note inviting him to make free use of the bath as often as he wanted to, adding that with six more girls in the house, she would have someone to help with the laundry, so he was welcome to add anything he wanted to the daily

Fight for the Future

wash. There, that should do it.

The bath was half full. She judged that when he got in, the water would just reach the overflow. Satisfied by another job well done, she skipped downstairs and was delighted to see that the kettle had just started boiling. She made tea, and put the now dry pots in the clean cupboard. There was almost nothing she enjoyed more than a plan coming together.

The door opened and Anthony walked in, looking cautiously at her. She smiled, and he smiled back, clearly puzzled by her good mood.

'Frannie's being nice. Enjoy it while it lasts. There's a bath waiting for you.' Eddie had his face buried in the *Daily Mirror*. He didn't look up.

'Thank you, Frannie,' Anthony said. He sidled past her, making directly for the bathroom. Two baths in just over a week. He sighed in anticipation.

He picked up her note and laughed, getting the message. He stripped off and got into the bath without testing the water. He yelped at the heat, and almost jumped out again, but settled back into it. The heat soothed his tired muscles, and he relaxed for a while before taking hold of the soap and flannel and cleaning himself thoroughly. He glanced at the shampoo at the side of the bath, and took a sniff. It was decidedly feminine, and he settled for washing his hair with the soap, rinsing it out with jugfuls of water from the cold tap.

With the bath clean, he reluctantly dressed in his soiled clothes, and went downstairs, sharing a silent meal with Eddie and Frannie. He got the feeling that they wanted to be alone, and left for his cabin. He left the door open. A slight breeze had started up, and he enjoyed the promise of rain in the air. He considered the pub, feeling his wages burning a hole in his pocket. Then he remembered the look of approval in Eddie's eyes when he'd talked about opening a bank account. He slipped the five single pound notes into his guitar case, drew out his guitar and started to play softly, crooning in a low, sweet voice. It would never have the raw power of Tomas's voice, but it was tolerable, he was sure. Next week he would buy the Everley Brothers record, but tonight he would pay tribute to 'the King'.

In the farmhouse, Frannie lifted her face from her knitting.

'Dad, turn the radio off,' she said quietly, moving to the window and opening it fully.

'What is it?'

'It's Anthony. Listen.' Her head was cocked to one side. She was smiling.

'What's that? I've heard it before.'

'Oh! It's "Don't be Cruel" by Elvis.'

Eddie kept a straight face. 'You like Elvis?'

'I *love* Elvis. I didn't know Anthony could sing as well as play guitar. Doesn't he sound wonderful? I'll ask him tomorrow if he wants to listen to some of my records.' Her thin face was lit up with enthusiasm. Eddie Shepherd watched her with a deep pleasure in his heart. There was almost nothing he enjoyed more than a plan coming together.

Chapter 8

The document was dated 1845. It was the title deed to the farm, accompanied by a copy of a will from Simon Harris, leaving the property to his nephew, Robert Shepherd.

Eddie wondered if they should really be in a bank vault, not this battered leather case, and yet where could he be more sure of them? He returned them to their envelopes. The farm had been a good living for his family for over a hundred years, but they'd never forgotten the previous occupants.

He picked up a few pages of lined foolscap, folded neatly in half. His own handwriting; again, he'd written down what his grandfather had told him.

> The first Shepherd to own this farm was Robert Shepherd. He got it from his mother's brother, Simon Harris, who had no children of his own. Simon Harris got it from his wife, Mary Verne that was, who was the last of the Vernes to die, and so the last one to own the land and the farm.
>
> The Vernes farmed this land for over two hundred years, and were known all around as fair people. They were good Christian people, and attended church regularly. My grandparents' generation and great-grandparents' generation remembered them well, and passed down stories.
>
> Some ask what they looked like – it's hard to say. They intermarried with the other

four families, and took in fosterlings so often from outside that nobody could say what the Verne look was, other than healthy. Then again, there's been many a time when healthy and well fed was such an unusual look that it was easy to spot someone from the Five Families, as they were called. Some were pale and red-haired, some were dark and dusky, like gypsies. Some were stocky and straw-haired. They were everything in between. The children grew taller than most, and were rarely pockmarked, or crippled. Some of them would grow up and marry outside the Five Families and it was always seen as a good thing, to be wed to one of them. The children of such a marriage often died young, and those that survived tended to be weak, but they were fiercely protected and often found their own marriages within the Five Families, when they were grown.

When the head of the family died, his whole generation would soon follow. You'd find that they had a few couples farming the land together, with their children. Well, that was what they gave out to be the case. If you looked at the children, you'd see that not all of them looked like the mother or father they were supposed to have. There were strong rumours of men taking more than one wife, aye, and worse, the women would take more than one husband. They were one big marriage, we reckoned, four or six or eight of them. The bonds were strong with them, and when one of the parents died, the other parents followed within a month or within a year. But there were always more to spring up, to fill their place.

They had few enemies locally – they did fair business with other families in the valley, and weren't known for extravagance. They were known to pay their debts on time. They rarely employed farmhands, or domestic help. Their own children were enough labour for their businesses and homes.

This is what I know about the people who had this farm.

Eddie carefully placed the document back in the file. 'Aye, we'll care for this land, this has been the Shepherd farm for over a hundred years,' he whispered. 'But I'm just one man, and it's so hard without Lily to help me.'

The brothers sat in the drawing room of the farmhouse. It was eight o'clock, two nights before the gig, and they were practising hard. There was a new Everly Brothers album out, and they'd been busy learning the songs. Tomas had scoffed at the idea of spending precious money on the sheet music, and they were picking it up by ear. Frannie had brought her record player downstairs. It had become an evening ritual for her and a couple of her sisters to play records while the twins listened carefully, making notes and strumming practice chords. Tomas was getting excited. 'Twenty pounds for one night's work. That's a tenner each. If we could do that every week we'd more than double our income.'

Anthony frowned. 'Let's get this one out of the way first. We have to do a good job if we want more bookings. Oh, bloody hell! Sorry, Frannie, pardon my filthy mouth.' A string had broken. He looked at it, dismayed.

'I've got a spare packet back at the Black Dog,' his brother offered.

'I've got spare strings, Tomas, what do you think I am? It's just more bloody— Sorry, Frannie ... more expense.'

Frannie was staring at him, outrage on her thin face.

He looked up. 'Come on, let's go to my cabin, Tomas. I can't work if I have to watch my mouth every sodding— I KNOW! ... every minute.'

Frannie glared at him. 'I don't like swearing in this house.'

'That's fine, because I won't be in the house,' he snapped back. Her face fell, and he closed his eyes, counting to ten.

'Frances, I'm sorry. It's what men do. It's stupid, and we shouldn't. I'm just tired, that's all.'

The next oldest sister, twelve-year-old Maisie, stood up. She had an open, pleasant face, and seemed to have inherited her older sister's share of good humour as well as her own.

'Frannie, me and Susan are going to bed. You and your boyfriend can argue just as well without us here.'

Frannie paled, and then blushed. 'He's not my boyfriend,' she said coldly. 'Why don't you just sod off and get bloody well lost.'

Tomas collapsed laughing, while Anthony almost broke his jaw struggling to keep his face straight. The older girl glared at them, and stalked out.

Ten-year-old Susan looked at the door, and then at the two young men.

'She's been in a foul mood all week. It's her birthday on Saturday, and she's got nobody to go out with.' On that note, she and Maisie left.

Tomas turned off the record player, reverentially putting the record back in the paper inner sleeve, then the cardboard outer cover. He looked up. 'Well, that's just wrong. Even for a skinny little wallflower wretch like Frances. All alone on her seventeenth birthday.'

'We've got the wedding gig that night. There's nothing we can do,' Anthony said dully.

'Hey, don't look so down, it's not your problem,' Tomas said. 'Did I tell you that Miriam knows the groom's family? She's got an invite, so she'll be coming. Why don't I ask her if Frannie can come too? That might cheer her up, and she might meet a nice bloke. A clerk, or a shoe salesman, or something. It's going to be a huge party, the bride's parents are loaded. They won't mind if Miriam brings a guest.' He laughed, a little cruelly. 'From the look of her, Frances doesn't eat much.'

Anthony looked down at his guitar,

unwinding the broken string. 'Leave her be.' His voice was quiet, calm.

Tomas glanced at him. 'Aw, all protective, eh? You've been here too long, you're going all big brother on these kids.'

Anthony looked up, met his twin's deep-brown eyes. They exchanged a long look.

'Oh,' said Tomas, utterly surprised. 'Why?'

'She's Dorothy Marsden's daughter, to start with. And she's absolutely wonderful, to finish with. And I'm going to marry her, and I'll be the best bloody husband in history.'

'Wow. That *will* surprise her.'

Anthony laughed, all seriousness suddenly gone. 'I know, that'll show her.' He stood up. 'I'll go after her. I'll invite her to the party. You go back to the pub, eh? I'll get nothing useful done tonight until I know she's OK.'

He went into the kitchen, looking for her. Tomas followed him, and left by the back door, smiling a knowing smile. Eddie was sitting at the table, reading the paper. He glanced up. 'Did I hear raised voices?'

Anthony met his gaze. 'You did, I'm afraid. Where is she? I'd like to apologise.'

'What have you done?' Eddie put the paper down. He was frowning.

'I swore. Then she got mad and swore back. And we laughed at her.'

'My Frances doesn't like bad language.' Eddie leaned back.

'I know. I think she's gone to her room. I

can't apologise if I can't speak to her.' Anthony stayed calm. He knew well enough not to seem too eager to see Frannie. Making it seem like a simple matter of courtesy to his employer's daughter was a wiser move.

'I'll drag her down,' muttered Eddie, folding his paper and leaving the kitchen. His tread on the stairs was heavy, tired. He returned within a minute.

'She's coming. She'll talk to you in the drawing room. Apparently.' He rolled his eyes to show his despair at the workings of daughters, and returned to his paper.

Anthony returned to the drawing room, and sat and waited. He felt absurdly formal. After fifteen minutes he stood and started to look at the photographs and paintings. A slight noise at the door made him spin round gracefully. He moved fast, and was just in time to catch her face change quickly from an appreciative smile to an angry frown. He was sure she didn't realise that she'd been caught out.

'Frances. I'm truly sorry. It won't happen again.'

'No? You're really saying that you'll never swear in front of me again?'

His lips twitched; he couldn't resist it. 'So long as you can make the same promise?'

Her eyes flashed with anger; she hated to be mocked. She looked at him for a long time before deciding that he wasn't being cruel. She relaxed a little. 'I accept your apology. And I promise I won't swear either. I know it's old-fashioned, but I like things to be nice. It's how I am.'

'I like how you are,' Anthony said quietly.

She looked up, certain now that she was being teased.

He kept his voice quiet, sincere. 'No, please believe me. I do. I know you think I'm good for nothing, but maybe one day you'll realise that I wouldn't hurt you for the world.'

'You like your music. I know that.' Her face lightened briefly.

'Yes. I take that very seriously. You know that gig I'm doing with Tomas? The wedding, on Saturday. Would you like to come? You've never seen us playing properly. And we couldn't have learned all these new Everly Brothers songs without your help. It would be a thank you, from us to you.'

Her eyes lit up, but then she frowned. 'I can't go to a wedding alone. And I'm sure that you're not supposed to bring a guest.'

'No, but Miriam is invited, and she would have taken Tomas as her guest. As he's already there, perhaps you could go with her? It's as good as sorted. He'll ask nicely, and she won't mind a bit.'

Frannie shook her head. 'No, thank you. It's kind of you, but I don't really know Miriam. It would be awkward.'

Anthony saw the problem immediately. 'Miriam's a handful, and I know she's got a bit of a reputation, but she's a kind soul really. I'm sure she'd love to introduce you to people. You wouldn't be alone. And I promise to keep an eye on you.' He hesitated. Was it too much? 'I really want you to be there.'

Fight for the Future

'Do you?'

'I can't think of anything I'd like more, right now.'

She stood up, her face dead straight. 'Are you asking me out?'

'I'd like to, but I'm scared of your dad's shotgun.' He flashed her his best smile.

'Ask him then. If he says it's OK, I'll go.' She left the room, shutting the door behind her. He heard her light footsteps as she ran upstairs, then the creak of her bed in the room above him. He picked his guitar up, turned off the lamps, and left the room.

In the kitchen, Eddie looked up. 'Has she calmed down?'

'I think so.' There was more than a trace of uncertainty in Anthony's voice.

'You're doing a better job than I've ever done then.'

'Eddie?'

'Hmmm?' The farmer's attention was on the crossword.

'I'll get the last chores done. OK? Check the stock, feed the cats.'

The farmer looked up. 'What are you after?'

Anthony allowed a smile to reach his eyes. 'Just permission to take your eldest to the wedding on Saturday night.'

'To cheer her up?' Eddie challenged.

'Not just that.' Anthony said. It was best to be honest.

Eddie put the paper down. 'It's like that, is it? I'm not sure. It's only a month since you and Linda

Jeanette Greaves

split up. And I know what happened after that.'

'I understand. All I can say is that you can trust me with her.'

'I'll believe you. And if I'm wrong, you'll lose your job, and your home. And I'll be waiting with a gun if you dare to show your face again around here.'

Anthony breathed out. 'You're not wrong.'

'Aye, well. It's her birthday too, make sure she has a good time.'

'I will,' Anthony promised.

Eddie waited until the young man had left, then rose to his feet. On the kitchen mantelpiece were several pictures of Lily. Almost hidden behind them was a picture of Dottie. It was a posed picture, in black and white. He picked it up and kissed it gently. 'I'm sorry, girl. I'll always be sorry. But I'm doing the best I can for our daughter.' He looked at the image for a while, before gently setting it down.

Chapter 9

At four o'clock on Saturday, Eddie found Anthony in the barn, sweating as he repaired a small hole in the roof. 'Hell's bells, lad. It must be ninety degrees up there. That's no job for August! 'Ave you not finished yet?'

'Nearly,' the young man called.

'Well, t'girl will be home soon, and she'll be taking over t'bathroom. Tha'd better get washed and dressed quick. I've just got back from town, picking up bits and pieces that she bowt at dinnertime. She couldn't get 'em back on her pushbike.'

'OK. Won't she be cooking before we go?'

'Nay, Maisie and Susan will do that. They're good girls. If I know my Frances, she won't want to eat. Make sure she has some of that buffet though. And don't encourage her to drink.'

Anthony slid down the ladder, braking with his hands and feet on the outside of the legs.

'Eh, that's a pretty trick. Where d'you learn that?' For a moment the farmer looked his age, open-eyed with pleasure at the farmhand's grace.

'Fastest way down. It's obvious.' Anthony looked at his employer with a puzzled frown.

'Fastest way to break your neck, more like. Did you hear what I said? About t'lass?'

Anthony looked solemn. 'If she looks anything more than tipsy, I won't let her have another drop.'

'Aye, good enough. What time will you be home?'

'Late.' Anthony looked guilty. 'I'm sorry, I know it's not good enough, but we've got to stay to the end. It's a wedding, and they'll want to dance.'

'Don't worry. It's her birthday, and she'll want to dance too. God knows she gets little enough chance. I'm not staying up. If the two of you aren't here in t'morning, I'll come looking for you.' The farmer's pale-blue eyes fixed on Anthony, and he didn't seem to be joking.

Anthony washed and dressed. He'd got pleasurably used to clean clothes. It didn't matter that they were second-hand. He could buy ten outfits from the second-hand shop for the price of one new one. His wardrobe was full. He and Tomas were copying the Everly Brothers' style as much as possible tonight. His hair was slicked back and looked, he thought, ridiculous. Still, it was what the customer wanted. One day they'd want his own music. Perhaps one day they'd want him…

He sat in the kitchen, holding his guitar loosely on his lap. He felt a sudden panic at the thought of hundreds of people watching him. He'd never remember the chords, the words. It was crazy to even think of learning three albums of someone else's music in three weeks. He took a deep breath and shut his eyes tight, fighting down nerves. When he opened them, Frannie was standing in the kitchen, looking at him questioningly.

'Have you changed your mind?'

'Almost,' he said, breathing out.

Her face froze, and she spun on her heel.

He laughed. 'I was talking about the gig. Not

you.'

She turned. 'Oh… You must think I'm stupid.'

'Yeah, right now I do.' He winked.

Something flickered in her eyes, a ghost of a tease. 'Well, I'm ready if you are,' she said.

He looked at her. She was wearing a long yellow printed skirt, slightly stained from a day in the cafe. Her white blouse was too big. Her black shoes were almost worn through, and her hair was tied back in a long, tight braid.

He smiled warmly. 'You look great. Let's go.'

She laughed. 'I was joking. How long have we got?'

'I'm due on stage at nine. Miriam's driving, she's got her dad's car. She'll pick us up at half seven.'

'So late?'

'So late,' he said gravely.

'Don't move,' she told him.

He was in the kitchen for what seemed like a lifetime, making small talk with Eddie, helping the little girls to cook. At precisely half past seven, Tomas knocked on the kitchen door. Anthony answered it, his guitar in his left hand. 'She's not quite ready,' he apologised.

'Yes, I am,' said a small voice behind him. Before he could turn, he felt a tiny hot hand take his. He looked for a moment into his brother's clear brown eyes, staring at the reflection of himself and his girl, hand in hand. Tomas blinked, and the spell was broken. Tomas bowed. 'Miss Shepherd. May we escort you to the dance?'

Jeanette Greaves

Her hand gripped his. Anthony could sense her nervousness, and he smiled. 'Tomas, the lady is with me. Do I try to steal your girl?'

He still didn't quite dare to look at her. When they eventually got to the car, he had the chance to step back and open the door for her. She looked anywhere but at him. He couldn't look anywhere but at her. For the first time he could remember, she was wearing something that fit her. It was a dark-red fitted dress, with a full skirt and off-the-shoulder short sleeves. He knew instinctively that it wasn't meant to be worn by a seventeen-year-old; the material was too rich, the cut too revealing. Amazingly, she was carrying it off. Her air of maturity, that seemed so eccentric in her ordinary life, gave her a power beyond her years. Her thick black hair was unpinned, but freshly cut. It fell shining and loose past her shoulders. She wore one item of jewellery, an antique gold and ruby necklace. She wore no make-up, she never did.

She glanced at him, before stepping into the car. He sat next to her, aching with pride. Miriam looked over her shoulder, and smiled encouragingly. 'You look fantastic, kid. Where the hell did *you* appear from? I didn't know I had this sort of competition around here!'

'I'm not here to compete with anybody,' answered the girl.

'Damn right, I think you've fought and won. I surrender! Just let me keep Tomas, and the rest of the world is yours.'

Frannie took Anthony's hand again.

'Do I look all right? I don't want to show you up. You've not said anything.'

He turned and looked at her properly for the first time. He tried to smile. 'I'm a bit speechless, that's all.'

'Oh. I'm sorry. I tried to put make-up on, but it made me look bad.'

'You tried to gild the lily. Or should I say paint the rose? Other women can only try to look like you do now. Cosmetics don't work for you because you're already beautiful.' He was keeping his voice down but Tomas, in the front seat, had overheard and was laughing. Anthony felt frustrated. Everything he said sounded like a cheap, overused line. He needed newly minted words to tell her how he felt.

They held hands all the way to the wedding. Anthony was content to just sit there, acutely aware of the steady pulse of blood through her wrist. He suddenly realised that he'd never held another hand for so long, so happily.

There was a brief silence when the group walked into the reception. Miriam disengaged herself from Tomas, and moved around to take Frannie's arm. She spoke in low and confidential tones to the girl. 'Yes, they're looking at us. Don't let it bother you. Raise your head. It's because I'm the trollop who dropped the doctor's son to take up with a no-good dago. And they really haven't a clue who you are, Cinderella, so let's have some fun until someone susses you. We're sitting at that table over there. I wangled it so that we would be close to the stage.

Here we go!'

The best man had risen from his seat, and was walking towards them. 'Good, you're here. Lads, you look great. Our blushing bride has been looking forward to this all day. Can you start with "Wake up Little Susie"?'

Miriam led Frannie to their table. She bitched happily, keeping her voice low. 'Typical, she's just got married, and all she can think of is Tom and Tony. Aren't we the lucky ones?' Frances bit the inside of her lip a little. The pain distracted her from the blush, and it faded almost as soon as it started. Anthony realised that she was gone, and hurriedly followed her to the table. He squeezed her hand, and then reluctantly let go.

'Frances, I've got to go. I'm here to work. You're here to have fun. Tell everyone it's your seventeenth birthday and let them spoil you. We're taking a break at ten thirty, for half an hour. There'll be food, and records, if you want to dance with me. Until then, I want to see you having fun. Miriam, don't corrupt her.'

Miriam looked at him and smiled. 'I know nothing that I could corrupt her with. Do I?'

The twins sat by the stage for a minute or two, tuning their guitars, checking with the best man about the set list. They took some notes, and then took to the stage.

Miriam sat down in a crowd of couples, moving bottles and glasses away to clear an empty space in front of Frannie's seat. Miriam was greeted merrily by the men and women, who all wanted to know who her friend was.

She introduced Frances to the crowd, who welcomed her without question. Any friend of Miriam's was fine with them, and most of them knew Eddie anyway. Slowly, Frannie started to relax, trying to tear her attention from the duo on stage enough to make conversation. After a while, she realised that she didn't have to try so hard. Fewer and fewer people were chatting, and more people were watching the twins. She glanced around the hall.

She knew it was wrong, and tried to signal to Anthony, but he was absorbed in the music. Tomas was surveying the crowd, enjoying being the focus of attention. She turned to Miriam.

'You have to speak to Tomas,' she said.

'What?'

'You've got to slow them down. This is bad.'

'Are you kidding? It's great? They're really rocking.'

'I know, but it's a wedding. Look at the bride. She's starting to get annoyed. She wanted background music from her favourite band, and instead the twins are stealing her show. They'll never get another wedding booking if they carry on like this.'

Miriam looked at her. 'You're a smart one, aren't you?'

'Just stop them,' Frannie said firmly.

Miriam stood up, and made her way to the stage. She waved to Tomas, feigning drunkenness. Frances knew that she'd had only one glass of champagne. People laughed, and started to chat again as Tomas stopped playing, and came to the front of the stage. He bent his head, and she whispered to him. His eyes took in the room, and he nodded.

He went back to his seat and took the mike again. 'It seems that my fiancée is my biggest fan. Well, I'll just say that I'm hers too, and then we'll get back to business. Could someone please get her a lemonade?' The guests laughed again, and he leaned across and whispered to his twin.

The set calmed down, the twins played well, but were more subdued, quieter. They played as if veiled. Conversation resumed and Frances looked around, satisfied. Miriam glanced at her with a new respect.

At half past ten a buffet was served, and someone started to play singles quietly. Frances took some food, filling a second plate for Anthony. He found her and led her to a quiet corner, gratefully taking the plate from her. A member of the groom's party brought him a pint, and he drank it back.

'It's a good job Miriam was here. We nearly blew it there. It didn't occur to me that we might be too good.'

Frances shook her head. 'No, I told Miriam to speak to Tomas. You need gigs like this to get money. I heard you speak to Tomas about it. It was me, not her.'

'Good for you. For seeing the problem, *and* for claiming credit,' he said approvingly. He hesitated, stuck for words again. 'I want to tell you how good you look, but anything I say would sound corny.'

Fight for the Future

'Do I look as good as you do?' she replied quickly, before she could think of what she was saying.

The young man was delighted. 'Oh now! Flattery and flirtation as well. I can't cope with this. I thought I was taking a little girl out for a birthday treat, and I've found myself outmatched.'

She didn't reply, but just looked at him. Why hadn't she noticed before that his eyes were the exact same shade as her own?

'How are you getting on with Miriam's crowd? Are they treating you OK?' He moved to a less risky subject.

'I'm holding my own, I think.'

'Good girl,' he said, hungrily biting into a sandwich.

She bristled up. 'Don't talk to me like that. As if I'm a child, or a pet.'

He frowned. 'Look, why don't you give me the rule book now? It will save time.'

'The rule book?'

He fought back a smile. 'You know, what I can and can't do.'

She shrugged. 'Sorry, you'll have to pick it up as we go along.'

Anthony seized on her words happily. 'As we go along? I like the sound of that.'

She surprised herself when she laughed. 'So do I. What about you? Do I need to know any rules?'

He opened his mouth to joke, and stood back in horror as he heard his stupid mouth run off without him. 'Just one rule: look as beautiful on our

Jeanette Greaves

wedding night as you do tonight.'

They stood and looked at each other, both of them fundamentally shocked at what he'd just said.

Frances recovered first. 'Anthony. There are some general boy–girl rules. I've read about them in magazines. My mum was very clear on telling me about them. Lily, I mean.'

Anthony nodded, still appalled at himself.

Frances spoke fast. 'Rules about what a nice girl shouldn't do on a first date. This is a first date, right?'

At that moment, Anthony was utterly sure that there would never be a second one.

Frannie continued. 'Well. It seemed to be an absolutely comprehensive list, but it didn't, anywhere, say that nice girls don't accept marriage proposals on a first date.'

She took two glasses of champagne from a passing waiter, and handed one to Anthony.

'I'm absolutely certain that the reason it's *not* on the list is because people who make those sorts of lists have no imagination. But still. It's not. I suppose it's a loophole.'

'What are you saying? This is getting very confusing,' admitted Anthony.

'I'm saying yes... Even though I'm only just seventeen. Even though I've only known you for a few months. Even though you've not kissed me yet, and I've spent the night wondering why you've not tried. Yes, I *will* marry you.'

She held the champagne glass to her mouth. 'Drink to it?' She took a sip.

He took a sip from his own glass, for luck, and then put the glass down.

'That kiss?'

'What about it?'

'May I?'

'You may.' She looked directly at him.

He leaned down a little. She wasn't much smaller than him. In her heels she was only a couple of inches shorter. His hands went to her waist, and he shivered as he felt the rich texture of the red cloth tight around her flesh. He let his hands fall to her hips, foreshadowing the complete possession that he was now sure of. She drew in her breath, and he stopped instantly, doing no more than pull her towards him. Her eyes were open, looking into his as he put his lips to hers, and kissed her gently, chastely. He reluctantly moved his hands away from her and put them behind his back, out of harm's way.

She sighed. 'Nobody's ever kissed me like that before.'

'I don't think I've ever kissed anyone like that before either.' He felt dizzy.

Tomas was there, suddenly, smiling. 'Stop canoodling, young lovers. It's time we were on stage again.'

Anthony scowled. 'I wanted that dance,' he told Frannie.

'There'll be other dances,' she said, putting her finger to her lips, and then to his. 'Do you have another break?'

'Midnight. The happy couple leave, and then we wind things down with a last set,' he told her.

'I'll see you then.'

The second set was for the bride. The twins played all her favourites, repeating one or two from the first set, at her request. Again, they kept it subdued, only breaking out freely and showing what they could do when the bride and groom took to the floor and danced.

At midnight, the newly-weds left in a shower of rice and good wishes, and someone started to play a Perry Como album quietly as the brothers jumped off the stage. The best man stood and announced that the party would go on, and the Preston Brothers would be back for a third set very soon. There was some enthusiastic applause from the younger guests, and Tomas flushed with pleasure. They found empty chairs and dragged them to the table, joining the women. Frances was completely at ease now, and was being gently sarcastic to a young man who was trying to impress her. The guy was too drunk to get the point, but trailed off in mid sentence when the dark-haired guitarist put his arm around Frannie's slim shoulders and smiled at him enquiringly. Anthony looked at his girl. Her throat was smooth and white, set off by the rubies, the dress, and her long black hair. He felt a mad urge to kiss it, in front of all these people, but contented himself with the new knowledge of how her hot skin felt under his light touch. She'd shivered when he'd put his arm around her, when he'd let his hand touch her upper arm. Somehow, they were making conversation when most of their consciousness was centred on where their bodies were touching.

Fight for the Future

Tomas was busy writing down names and numbers. Anthony suddenly realised that his brother was taking bookings, working hard. He excused himself to Frannie and leaned across to speak to Tomas. 'Need any help?'

'No, you relax. You look like you need a rest.'

There was a wicked glint in Tomas's eye, and Anthony grinned. When they took to the stage again most of the guests had gone, leaving just the younger crowd behind. They picked up their guitars and took their seats, looking around.

'More Everlys?' asked Tomas, smiling at the forty or so people who were left.

'Can you do Elvis?' called out a pretty blonde.

'Better than *he* can.' Tomas winked, and Anthony strummed a couple of chords for emphasis. He was laughing. This was so much better than folk singing in the Black Dog. He was achingly aware that he wanted to do this more than almost anything else in the world. He knew they were better than most of the music in the charts, but they were trapped, they couldn't ever reach for the success that they deserved. This kind of thing was OK, but they needed to keep a relatively low profile. There was deadly danger out there, and he could never be allowed to forget it. He glanced up and looked at Frances, realising that she was awake on adrenaline alone. She'd been up early to make the family breakfasts, and had spent the day working at the cafe, and shopping for her dress. She'd been awake for over twenty hours, and was beginning to look very tired. Miriam's day had been much less tiring, and she was eager for more. Anthony gave his directions to his twin. 'Three fast, for dancing, then a couple to wind down. It's late.'

'OK, will that leave them happy?'

'They're already happy. Just let them dance.' The brothers shared a smile.

'I wish we had a drummer,' Tomas said wistfully.

Anthony dismissed the sentiment. 'We haven't. Everlys and Elvis. OK?'

They played 'Hound Dog' and 'Jailhouse Rock', and then fumbled their way convincingly through a request that Tomas sing the Bobby Darin hit, 'Dream Lover'. Miriam actually blushed when he sang it. She recovered, and called out 'Frankie Lymon!'

'OK,' sighed her fiancé, resigned. 'I hate this song, but the lady wants it.' He winced a little, but made a good job of 'Why do Fools Fall in Love'. The applause came, together with some good-natured joking about the particular fools in question, but the song wasn't popular, and people started to drift away. Miriam beckoned to Tomas, and he started to stand. Anthony looked up.

'Hey, I learned this, and we've not played it.'

Tomas paused, and picked up his guitar again. 'Dream?'

'Yeah.' Anthony looked down, and cleared his throat. The brothers sang their favourite Everly Brothers song, which hadn't been requested all night. They finished with a shared smile. It had come

Fight for the Future

together beautifully.

They looked up. The steward of the hall was standing by the locked bar, waving his keys at them.

'OK, we're off.' Tomas laughed. While they'd been playing quietly, singing almost to each other, the rest of the guests had gone to collect coats and bags, and had taken the hint, filing out of the room.

'I'll drive,' called out Tomas to his fiancée. 'You're tired.'

'You've got to be joking. When did you get your licence?' she demanded.

'I've got all the licence I need,' he said, flirting.

Anthony grabbed his guitar case and packed his instrument away carefully. 'Did we get paid?' he asked, frowning.

'Oh yes. Here.' Tomas reached into his pocket and took out two five-pound notes. 'I've got four more bookings. We're on our way to fame and fortune.'

He registered the alarmed expression on Anthony's face and shrugged. 'OK, we'll settle for fortune. Come on kids, we're going home.'

Chapter 10

Eddie made his way downstairs at six o'clock, surprised to hear the kettle whistling on the hob, and to smell breakfast almost cooked. He peered around the kitchen door and nodded at Anthony, who was flipping fried eggs over in a pan. The young man looked up. 'I let myself in. She had a tiring day yesterday. I thought I'd make our breakfast.'

Eddie frowned at him, and Anthony spoke defensively. 'I'll get the milking done, I just thought I'd make our breakfast so that she doesn't have to get up early. Nobody else has to be up until eight anyway. You don't mind?'

'Nay, she's not the world's greatest cook. Did she have a nice time?'

'Yes, I think so.' Anthony was cautious. The sound of light feet on the stairs made him go still, and the intent look on his face when Frannie peered around the door reassured Eddie. Anthony went straight to her side.

'Frances, why don't you have a lie in? You had to work on your birthday, so today I'm going to do all your jobs. I'm sure your dad won't mind.'

Eddie spoke up. 'Aye, back to bed little 'un. It's reet. It's time Maisie started pulling her weight a bit more. You rest.' He shook his head as Frannie smiled her thanks at both men, and climbed the stairs again. Eddie reflected on how tired she seemed. In his mind's eye he pictured her holding on to the bannister as she made her way back to bed. He filled two pint mugs with tea and shoved one across the table to Anthony.

'So you keep her out to an ungodly hour, then treat her like royalty? I take it you two had fun last night.'

'Fun? Well, we...'

Eddie stared at him. 'Yes?'

'We sort of agreed that we want to be a couple.' Anthony managed to say. In the morning light, he was daunted by the thought of explaining to Eddie that he and Frances were unofficially engaged.

'Well, don't be scared of me, lad, it's fine by me. At least I can keep an eye on you, with you living on my farm. Are you serious?'

'Very,' said Anthony.

'In that case, you'd better wash this lot up before Maisie gets up. Then the milking, then you can make a start on cleaning the drawing room. Then the little girls need to be woken up, and got ready for chapel. Maisie and Susie will help you with that. I'll wake Frannie up before Sunday dinner. When you get back from chapel you can help her with that.'

'Chapel?' said Anthony, horrified.

'Aye, if you're serious, you'd better start getting your face seen at chapel. Well, what are you waiting for?'

Anthony sprang to his feet with a grin, and started to wash up. Eddie pulled his wellies on, and went to check his stock.

Eddie unhitched the pony and let it loose to graze on the sweet grass outside the orchard walls. The plums and damsons were ripe and the crop was a good one. His second eldest daughter, Maisie, was already scooting around the orchard, picking up windfalls and carrying damaged or rotting fruit well outside the walls for the wildlife and the butterflies, as her mother had taught her years ago.

'Watch out for wasps,' Eddie called out. Maisie looked up and smiled. She'd always loved this job. She'd been coming out with Eddie and her mum since she was a little ' un, but this was her first harvest without her mother, and she was obviously thinking about years past.

'Mum always got stung' ,she said.

'Aye, and she didn't care, said it was good for the blood. Eddie smiled back. Don't worry about separating damsons and plums, we'll do that when we get back. Just get them in the baskets, cover them up, and put them on the pony trap.'

Maisie gave him her best 'I know what I'm doing' look, and settled to the task. When she'd picked up all the windfalls she switched to picking the low-hanging fruit while her dad went for the higher fruit, using a curved cane to drag down the higher branches. 'Remind me, Maisie, I need to prune these at the end of the harvest, they're getting a bit high for me.'

'Why's there an orchard here?' Maisie asked. 'Irene Shuttleworth says that you should put the orchard near the farmhouse, not on the other side of the farm.'

'She said that, did she?' Eddie thought for a minute. 'Well, it's here because the bricks were here, for the wall.'

'Why were the bricks here?'

'Because the old farmhouse was here, on this side of the farm. Before the Shepherds came here.'

'The Vernes?'

'Aye.' Eddie nodded. What do you know about the Vernes?'

'They had this farm for hundreds of years, before we had it. And they died, nearly all of them, at the same time.'

Eddie sighed. 'Aye.'

'Where did they die?'

'Mostly in the farmhouse.'

Maisie digested the information, and then looked round, eyes wide. 'So, here? They died here?'

'Aye, right here. Our family knocked it down, and used the bricks to build walls for an orchard.'

'And the bodies?' Maisie was fascinated.

'The bodies are in the graveyard, in St Thomas's, over towards Kendal. We didn't have a chapel back then.'

'Were they murdered?'

'That's a story for when you're older. And don't look at me like that, nobody's going to come and kill us. It was a long time ago, and the world was different. And if you eat one more of them plums you'll have a runny arse for a week, I promise you.'

Maisie laughed and put the plum in the basket. 'Will we make jam?'

Jeanette Greaves

'Jam, and crumbles, and pies, and some we'll just stew and have with cream.'

Maisie nodded, and got on with picking the plums. Eddie suppressed a sigh. Not all the bodies were in the graveyard, according to the stories. His thoughts went back to a day in the orchard, spent with his grandad, when he was much the same age as Maisie.

'Most of t'stories are forgotten. Don't go tellin' tales, but you need to know, because someone has to pass 'em down, generation to generation. I never told your dad, because he were a blabbermouth, but you're a quieter type, Edward, and you'll remember t'Vernes without telling t'world about them.

'This orchard is on t'site of t'auld farmhouse. The bricks in the walls are from that house, and the lintel over the gate is from t'kitchen door. After the Vernes were killed, there was no way anyone were living in that house. The smell of blood was bad, and everyone said it would never go away. I was told that it ran in rivers out of t'doorway.

'There were three dozen bodies buried, parents and bairns, grown-up children who had stayed around, fosterlings and a couple of wives and husbands from the village who had married into the family. There were other bodies there, of strangers – white-haired young men who had come to kill, and had died doing their bloody work. They were buried at the crossroads, as was the custom for murderers.'

Fight for the Future

Eddie still remembered how his grandad had paused and stared at him.

'You're a steady sort, aren't you?'

'Aye,' Eddie had said, all serious.

'Well, and I promise you that this is true, there were other bodies in the house, and us Shepherds buried them. But they weren't human bodies. They were wolves, big and strong, bigger than any dogs you've ever seen.'

'Wolves. The white-haired men brought wolves?'

'They *were* the wolves.' Grandad had nodded. 'And so were t'Vernes. I don't know what the quarrel was, but it was a bad one, and not one that anyone else but the Five Families were party to. Because they all died, that night. Every man, woman and child in the Five Families. Some wives and husbands who'd married in were spared. The children weren't. It was a horror, but if you look for reports you won't find them, because those bodies, the bodies of the wolves – nobody could explain them. The church records say the plague killed those families, but there was no plague back in the 1830s, not here anyway. Us Shepherds know the truth. We were their neighbours, you know?'

Eddie shook his head. 'You're joking with me.'

I am not.' Grandad shook his head. 'And don't even mention this to your mum. Where do you think they buried the wolves?'

Eddie looked round.

'Aye, right here, and built a wall around them, and planted the fruit trees over them. When I was a young man, I took up a dying apple tree, and a wolf skull came up with the roots.' Grandad took note of Eddies wide eyes. 'Aye, and I buried it again right away, but if you need me to prove it to you, we could take a spade to this whole place, we'll turn up wolf bones within a few minutes, I reckon.' Eddie still remembered his grandad's hard stare, and the emphatic prod to the ground that the old man had made with his stick. After Grandad passed away, Eddie had made his way to the orchard one day, and taken a spade to the rich earth. He had to dig deep, but seven or eight feet down were bones aplenty. Farm boy that he was, he knew the skulls weren't sheep or cattle or pigs, killed and buried in some long ago outbreak of disease. He climbed out of the pit and filled it in again. It was autumn, the leaves were falling, and his work was hidden by fallen leaves.

Chapter 11

Anthony was working in the lane, driving in posts for a new fence. The old one was nothing but rotten sticks, and he had pulled it apart. It would do as firewood. He'd treated the new wood himself, and was enjoying the fact that Eddie had let him take on the fencing project completely. As he stood back to survey the line of the first twenty posts, he realised that the sun was high in the sky, and that he was hungry. He sat down in the shade of a large sycamore, and took out his lunch.

The three apples were wizened but sweet, almost the last of the previous year's supply from the farm's small orchard. He ate one straight away, chasing it down with a long swig from a glass bottle of dandelion and burdock. He enjoyed the rich flavour of the dark drink. He had the heel of a loaf to go with a chunk of Lancashire cheese and a couple of slices of thick-cut ham. He stared dolefully at the bread – dense, grey and stodgy – and then looked around carefully. Nobody was looking, so he ripped it into small pieces and scattered it for the birds. He wrapped the cheese in the ham, and wolfed it down, taking another swig of the drink, bolting down the last two sweet apples, and carefully saving the rest of the pop for later.

By mid afternoon the posts were in, and he was ready for the cross planks. They were stacked up against the barn, and he would need to bring them down in the cart. As he made his way back, he glanced over to the lane. A glint of sun on metal drew his eye to the slight figure of his beloved, pushing her bike to the gate. He broke into a run and was at the gate before she was, holding it open and grinning broadly.

'Have you had a wonderful day?' he asked.

'Fantastic. There's nothing like spending the warmest hours of a summer's day in a pub kitchen to make me feel sparkling and energetic,' said Frannie drily. 'And you should put your shirt on, you'll get sunburned.'

'Tanned. Not burned. It may not mean much to you pasty Lancastrians, but I like being this colour. I like the way my skin smells.' He pulled his shirt on nevertheless.

Frannie blushed a little. She was walking close enough to him to pick up the clean smell of sun-warmed flesh, and was uncomfortably aware that she smelled of kitchens and dry sweat. She promised herself a quick drenching in the new shower when she got home, and a change of clothes. Anthony didn't seem to mind though. He'd gently relieved her of the bicycle, and was pushing it one handed. His other arm was casually round her shoulder. She moved slightly closer to him. They'd still not spoken to her father about their engagement. Two days after the party, Anthony had nervously broached the subject with her, and both of them had been relieved to find that the other hadn't seen it as a party-night joke.

'When are we going to tell him?' asked Anthony suddenly.

Frannie jumped. She'd been daydreaming.

Fight for the Future

'Who?'

'Your dad. About us getting married.'

'Oh. Soon. He's just about got used to me having a steady boyfriend though. Let me decide, eh?'

'Whatever you say, my love.'

'My love,' Frannie echoed.

'Are you laughing at me?' Anthony sounded offended, but when she looked up at him, he was smiling.

'Not right this minute, no. I like it when you say that.'

'It's true. Can I have a kiss before we go inside?'

Frannie looked round. Six younger sisters made it difficult to conduct a love affair with someone who practically lived with her. She decided that they were unobserved, and then drew Anthony into the shadow of the barn.

'Just one, then I'm sure you've got things to do,' she said, raising her face to him and closing her eyes. She waited to be kissed ... waited a little more, and then opened her eyes. 'What are you waiting for?' she said crossly.

Anthony smiled mischievously. 'I just like to see you with your eyes closed, that's all.' He bent and kissed her gently, his hands light on her shoulders. She never knew what to do with her hands when he kissed her like that. She wanted to touch him, but was scared to. She enjoyed the kisses; they made her feel safe and wanted, and beautiful. Lost in a reverie, she realised that his hands had moved from her shoulders to her waist, and that he was close to her, their bodies almost touching. She hissed, and he backed off. He blinked, then turned away.

'I'm sorry,' she whispered.

'It's OK. I know. You want to wait until we're married. But Frannie, it's just a kiss.' He struggled to hide his frustration, not for the first time wondering if he should have fought harder for Miriam. Tomas was strutting around the village like a young tomcat, and everyone knew why. Anthony shook his head and dismissed the thought. Now that he knew her better, he liked Miriam well enough, but every day he was falling more deeply in love with Frances.

He sighed and changed the subject. 'What are you doing this afternoon?'

'I was going to get changed, then do some baking. We're out of bread.'

He hid his expression, and then brightened. 'I was going to take a break, get back to the fencing after tea, when it's cooler. Why don't we make the bread together?'

Frannie wrinkled her nose. 'It's hard work, and it's boring. I hate doing it. And my bread isn't as nice as Mum's used to be.'

He followed her into the farmhouse, and absently started to tidy up while she showered and changed. She came downstairs wearing an old red blouse of Lily's, and an old, knee-length black skirt. He stared at the sweet shadow of the hollow behind her knee. The blouse was several sizes too big, and drowned her, hanging halfway down the skirt, hiding her slight figure. Her hair was still wet, and she'd plaited it into pigtails. He thought longingly of the night of her birthday, the first and last time he'd seen her wear anything that fitted her properly.

She stood on tiptoe to reach on to a high shelf for a large mixing bowl, and then got flour and yeast out of a cupboard. She poured the flour into the bowl, and mixed some yeast powder into it before going to the tap to get some water. She looked over her shoulder.

'What are you frowning at?' she snapped.

'Well, I remember my mum making bread, and she didn't do it like that.' His face was a picture of perplexity.

Frannie scowled. 'Look. All I know is that nobody's ever shown me how to do it. They just assume that I know. I was off school ill when we did bread in domestic science. Can you do any better?'

He rolled up his sleeves and went to the sink, washing his hands and lower arms thoroughly. Frannie stared in fascination at the way his muscles moved under his tanned smooth skin. She turned away quickly as he shook his hands dry and wiped them on a clean tea towel.

He indicated the mess of yeast and flour. 'Right, chuck this out. Now, get a pint of water in the kettle and warm it up. Don't boil it, we need it warm, but not hot enough to burn.' She did as he asked, and then looked at him as he shook out the yeast granules. 'Yeast is alive. This dust is asleep, that's all. We need to wake it up, so it will raise the bread. It needs a bit of sugar, and some nice warm water to wake it up gently.'

Jeanette Greaves

She was watching him carefully. He was absorbed in the task, trying to remember the steps his mother had gone through every morning. Usually, she'd been shouting at his father about something at the time. He dismissed the thought – it was too painful when he didn't know if they were safe – and continued, taking fresh flour and weighing out about a pound and a half, sieving it into the bowl with a teaspoon of salt.

'Salt,' muttered Frannie. 'Of course! I've never put salt in! I'm useless.'

He looked up quickly. 'Never,' he said, with utter conviction, before returning to the task. He took the kettle off the heat, and poured the water into a bowl. He checked it with a finger, and hissed. 'Too hot. Feel this. It won't hurt, I promise.'

Frannie put her finger in the water. 'What now?'

'I'll wait for it to cool. Then I'll put the yeast in the water. That's what Mama did.'

They sat and looked at each for a few minutes, then Anthony dipped his finger in the water again. 'Perfect, try that. All warm and welcoming for the little yeasties,' he said.

She looked at him suspiciously, and then tried the water. 'OK, I can remember that. What now?'

'Now we mix the flour and the yeasty water.'

'I can do that,' she said stiffly, reaching for a wooden spoon. He stopped her.

'Just a minute. You use that one for everything. It will taint the bread with other flavours. For today, it will have to do, but we'll buy some new ones, and keep one just for bread. OK?'

'OK.' She smiled. She liked that 'we'. She started to mix the flour and water together, struggling with the stiff mixture. As the dough bound together, Anthony told her to put the spoon aside and use her hands. At last she had it all bound together in one glistening lump in the bowl, with no flour at the sides. She smiled in satisfaction. 'Now, that's how it usually looks, more or less,' she challenged him.

'It's what's going on inside that matters.' He leaned across and kissed her on the forehead.

'Now, we knead it,' he said.

'I know,' she muttered. He watched her as she put the dough on the table and moved it about a little.

'Knead it!' he exclaimed.

'I am doing!' she retorted.

'Woman, you're playing with it! It needs air. That's what you're trying to do, put air in it for the yeast to breathe. It's not symbolic, you need to fold air into it, punch air into it.'

'Anthony, it's heavy,' she pointed out.

'It's bread! How are you going to cope with a baby if you can't lift bread?'

She fell silent. In a fury she stormed out of the room.

Anthony waited until she was out of earshot, and then swore inventively. He followed her upstairs and knocked on her bedroom door.

'Come downstairs, please,' he said.

'You can't tell me what to do,' she said glacially from inside the room.

111

'And *you* can't walk out on me like that. It's rude, and I don't like it.'

She opened the door and stared at him. He was leaning back against the wooden landing railings, his eyes open and quizzical. 'Are you coming or not? Because if you don't, I won't even try to teach you anything, ever again.'

She was immediately sure that he meant it. He was like her father in that, in his honesty. She shrugged. 'Will you stop criticising me?'

'It's teaching, not criticising. How else will you learn? And I'm sure you've got things to teach me, so it goes both ways. Are you coming downstairs?'

'OK,' she grumbled. He walked downstairs behind her, watching that unnervingly erotic play of muscles in her lower legs again, sighing as she returned to the bread.

'Right, now take it out on the bread,' he told her, watching with satisfaction as she thumped and pummelled the dough. After three minutes, she looked up at him with delight.

'It feels almost alive,' she said, laughing.

'Good. Now, we'll let it rest for a couple of hours. We'll put it near the range, in that big bowl, and wrap the bowl with a clean wet cloth.'

'I know this bit,' she said. She went to kiss him, to his surprise. 'Thank you. I should have paid more attention to Mum when she was making bread. I always had my head in my homework though.'

Anthony finished wrapping the bowl and popped it next to the range. He sat on one of the kitchen chairs and looked at her. She was standing at the sink, leaning against it. There was an unaccustomed flush of pleasure on her face. It suited her, and he didn't want to see it go.

'Did you enjoy school? I never went. My parents taught me to read and write, and my numbers.'

She was enthusiastic. 'Really? You poor thing! I loved school, well, the lessons anyway. Some of the other children were horrible. I like maths and English and geography and history. I wish I had time to read more now.'

Anthony nodded; he knew she had a thirst for knowledge. 'When we've got our own house, we'll have lots of books. We'll have a set of encyclopaedias. I'll buy them for you as a wedding present.'

Her eyes lit up. 'That's brilliant. I'd rather have that than almost anything. I would have carried on at school, you know? Like Linda did. I could have gone to the sixth form, and university, but when Mum died, I had to look after Dad. I've missed my chance now.'

He didn't argue, he couldn't. 'You're wasted in that kitchen, and that cafe. You should get a job where you can use your brain a bit more.'

She opened her mouth to protest, and then looked at him. 'Maybe I can. I took those jobs because of the hours, because Dad needed me on the farm. But you're here now, and Maisie and the others are getting bigger. Maybe I could get a different job. Maybe I could start putting something in that building society account for our house? The house that we're going to have lots of books in.'

Their eyes met, and she crossed the room, taking a chair next to him, and resting her head on his shoulder. They sat in the warm kitchen for long minutes, the rich yeasty smell of the rising bread filling the room. Neither of them wanted to break the silence. Anthony ached to touch her, to make further claims against her promise to him, but hesitated in the face of her inexplicable fear of contact. He'd never found himself in this situation before, and although he was willing to wait until their marriage to make her his, he was getting increasingly concerned by the way she was with him. She drew back at the slightest contact, and although he was sure she enjoyed his kisses, she would not allow the caresses he longed for. He'd seen her look at him, when she thought he was unaware of her regard, and was certain that she found him attractive. She was driving him mad. As usual, her very presence was arousing him, and eventually he got to his feet. 'I'm going to get the eggs in,' he explained. She sat up, blinking. 'Of course. Shall I help you?'

'No, that henhouse stinks. That's the next big job, cleaning that out properly. I'll do it.'

As he left the kitchen, Eddie passed him in the doorway. The two men grunted at each other in greeting. Eddie took a deep breath, and stared at his daughter.

'The bread smells different,' he commented, cautiously.

'Well, let's hope it tastes better than before...'

Frannie's tone was caustic, and he smiled at her ruefully. 'Well, I didn't want to say anything, you were trying so hard.'

She looked at him fondly. 'Dad, you should have said something. I knew it was awful, you know?'

He sighed as his pulled his boots off. 'I don't doubt it. Anyway, who taught you to do it properly?'

'Anthony,' she said. She sounded surprised by the question, as if it was self-evident that all good things came from Anthony. Her father smothered a smile and looked at her.

'Ah well, he'll want a wife who can make bread. Have you lovebirds set a date yet?' he teased.

She jumped guiltily, and he stared at her. 'Frances? Have you got something to tell me?'

'Well, we were going to tell you. We are going to get married. When we've got enough money saved up for a deposit on a house.'

For a second, he sat there with his mouth open, then he opened his arms. 'Come here you daft beggar. Give me a hug. Are you sure about this?'

She looked at him as if he'd gone mad. 'Of course I'm sure. It's Anthony. You like him, I like him, the girls like him. Everybody likes him. I don't see why he likes me, but I'm not going to worry about that too much.' She went to him, and sat on his knee – forgetting that she was seventeen and engaged – being, for a few moments, his little girl. His complicated, bad-tempered, fragile little girl. His heart almost missed a beat. He'd had his suspicions about Anthony's sudden and intense interest in her, but wisely kept quiet. He was sure, by now, that

Anthony's feelings for the girl were real. There was no point in stirring up trouble.

'Bless you, sweetheart, that's the best news I've had for years. You don't have to worry about the wedding. I've got insurance policies for all you girls, you know. And there's a bit put aside from your mother as well, for when you do get married, for your own home. I was going to give it to you when you turned twenty-one, but that might be a bit late.'

Frannie jumped off his lap. 'Really? How much?' She was unnervingly direct at times.

'Enough that you won't have to try too hard to get a mortgage. You can get married as soon as you're eighteen if that suits you? Not that I'd stand in the way if you wanted to wed sooner, of course.'

'Oh Dad! That's brilliant. It's not tied up in the farm, is it? I don't want to leave you in any trouble.'

He shook his head. She had a good business sense, and had been doing his accounts since Lily died. 'Nay, it's in a separate account. Nice interest rate too, it's grown a fair bit. It's in your name.'

She kissed him on the cheek. 'Dad? Can I tell Anthony? Can I tell him now?'

'Aye, I'm pretty sure by now he's not after you for your money.' He glanced at her, dressed in a five-year-old skirt and a hand-me-down blouse. Unusually, she didn't pick up on his sarcasm, and ran out of the kitchen door.

He heard her talking excitedly. Then Anthony came into the kitchen, carrying a basket of eggs. He put them carefully by the sink to be washed,

Fight for the Future

and then sat down. Frannie was still chatting excitedly, and he raised his hand. 'Hush, my love, please?' Frannie quietened, still smiling, and stood behind him, her arms around his neck. He reflected that she'd never done that before. He looked at Eddie.

'I should have asked permission to propose.'

'Can't be helped sometimes,' said the farmer. 'Frannie deserves some romance, it was more than her poor mother got.'

Anthony licked his lips. He was trying to be diplomatic. 'Eddie. This money that you say is Frannie's. I would like to see the account book now, please.'

Eddie nodded. It was clear that Anthony suspected Eddie of trying to find a way of giving them money. Anthony would have refused an outright gift. 'I suppose if I can't produce it right away, you'll say you can't accept it. You're a good lad, Anthony. It's true though, she's got money of her own. I'm not making it up.'

He went to the drawing room and emerged with a small hardback building society passbook. He handed it to Frannie.

'There you go. It will make a nice big deposit. You can spend your savings on furnishing your house then. And I'm paying for the wedding, I won't hear any arguments there. I've got a policy for that.'

'Dad. I love you,' said Frannie.

Anthony cleared his throat. 'This changes things. Tomas and Miriam are getting married in April. We don't want to steal their thunder, so I suggest sometime after June. What do you think?'

'The second of September. The first Saturday after my 18th birthday,' said Frannie confidently. Anthony stared at her and she explained. 'I always know what day of the week a date will be. It's just a thing.'

They both looked at Eddie.

'You'll carry on working for me, Anthony? And Frannie will do my accounts still?'

'Of course,' they promised.

'Then fine. One other thing. Anthony, you need to start going to chapel every Sunday, or the vicar will sulk.'

'I can do that,' promised the farmhand. 'Right. That bread will be ready for another thrashing in about half an hour. I'll clean these eggs up.'

They were interrupted by the intense din of six girls getting home from school and nurseries, the oldest pushing the youngest in prams. The adults fell silent, and concentrated on getting the tea ready. Soon after, Anthony showed Frannie how to deal with the bread again. She left it to rise for another hour, writing down his instructions.

Anthony kissed her lightly, and went out to work on the fence.

Dusk came late, and when he got back to the farmhouse all the lights were out, and everyone was in bed. He brushed his teeth at the outside tap, and went back to his cabin. Sitting on the bed, wrapped in a blue ribbon, was a small crusty loaf of white bread. He sat down and ripped off a crust, tasting it tentatively. He could vaguely taste lamb, and

Fight for the Future

reminded himself to buy new wooden spoons next time he was shopping. Otherwise it was delicious. He ate his fill, and went to sleep.

Chapter 12

The black wolf trotted inside the fence lines of the farm, leaping over stiles. The cattle lowed nervously, but didn't run. They had got used to him. He paused regularly; the fence had been marked on the opposite side here and there by dogs out for walks with their owners. He resisted the urge to cover the marks – although he didn't expect trouble, it would be foolhardy to advertise his presence.

In the small orchard, close by the fence, a vixen popped her head up then disappeared underground. The wolf pricked up his ears with interest, and approached the den. There was room on the farm for one vulpine family. The wolf and the farmer were agreed on that. This was the third pair to find the den that summer. The other families had been driven away when they paid too much attention to the henhouse, and not enough to the field mice and the rats. This pair seemed to have some intelligence, and had kept away from the stock.

He went back to the fence line, and started to run, stretching his muscles, putting all his energy into pushing himself, faster and faster, the world a blur, the worries of human life fading away in the sheer pleasure of running beneath the moon. He was young and fit, and king of his world. He was lost in the sheer fun of it when something fast, solid and large broadsided him from the left, knocking him over into the fence. He twisted around frantically, scrabbling against the fence for purchase, finding his feet and springing up, looking around. A pair of clear yellow eyes shone from the darkness, and the black wolf stood stock still, sniffing the air. He relaxed, and bowed down on his front legs, stretching them in front of him, lowering his head playfully. The second wolf advanced, stiff-legged, growling. It came in low, going for his throat, and he turned away at the last possible second, leaping back, taking stock, and going for the neck bite. He let his teeth penetrate the skin, just a fraction, before drawing back and glaring at his brother. Tomas yelped and then changed, rubbing at the back of his neck.

'What was that for?' Anthony demanded.

'We're getting too comfortable here. I thought I'd remind you how a wolf really fights,' Tomas growled. 'Turns out you didn't need the reminder.'

Anthony licked his lips. 'Mum used to do that, just leap out at us when we weren't expecting it, and if we didn't fight back for real we'd be in such trouble.'

Tomas snorted. 'She broke my leg once. I'd only been changing for a month or so, and wasn't really in charge of my wolf body. She bit my thigh so hard she cracked the bone. I changed back with the leg still broken and she had to take me through the change twice more until I came back healed.'

'Same with me, but my arm.' Anthony said. He shook his head. 'So many kids she had, and she brought all of us up knowing how to fight for our lives. She's a tough one.'

'It's been seven years. I'd love to see her and Papa again. I bet our sisters are changing now, they're old enough.'

'Yeah. Best not. You know what Papa said about his parents – one of his own brothers was being watched by the White Pack and led them back to the family home. Only Papa survived, because he was in town shopping. He heard the news and just got on the next coach out of town. Once we've left home, we can never go back. Not until the Whites are gone.'

'There's too many of them for us to take on alone.' Tomas looked angry.

'So we regroup, and find more of their enemies, and try to win the small battles as they come.' Anthony shrugged. 'But for now, we hide, and we stay vigilant.'

Tomas breathed deeply. 'Miriam is pregnant.'

Anthony let loose a low exclamation of delight. 'Tomas, that's brilliant!'

'Brilliant? We're not married yet! And that bastard of a vicar has made it clear that he doesn't like me. He's said that the earliest date that he can manage is January. She'll be showing by then, and she's furious about it. Anyway. We'll have to have a quiet registry office wedding. Her dad is ready to disown her. He thinks we've both proved him right. We're getting married in three weeks, in Lancaster. Will you and Frances be witnesses?'

'Frannie can't. She's still underage. Has Miriam no friends who will?'

'No, half of them have suddenly decided they'd rather hang out with Jennison and his new fiancée. Miriam's spitting feathers because he's going out with a 'Lady'. Some horsey type he met at university. Anyway, we're out of favour. Being the life and soul of the party is one thing; being pregnant is another, it seems. The other half of her friends think I've led her astray, and she's fallen out with them. That's funny, she's the one leading *me* astray half the time.'

Anthony rolled his eyes. Tomas gave him a wise look. 'Thanks for not telling me about that, by the way.'

'What?' his twin asked cautiously.

'About Miriam coming on to you. She confessed in a weepy fit last week. She confessed to an awful lot. God Almighty, I love that woman, but she's hard work. You should be glad you don't have to spend every minute watching Fran flirting with every man she sees.'

Anthony gave a short, cynical laugh. 'At least you're getting laid! I'm ready to explode. Nine more months of this and I'll have forgotten how to!' He smiled at the sound of his twin's dirty laugh.

'Hey, Anthony, if you forget how to, I'll help out with Frannie.'

Anthony looked sideways at Tomas. 'You and Miriam deserve each other. I'll stand for you at the wedding. I'm sure Eddie will too. I'll ask him.'

'Eddie?'

'Yeah. He'll understand. Come round tomorrow, in daylight, and ask him. Where will you live?'

'Ah, there's an empty flat above the chippy. We've asked about renting it for a while. It won't be nice, but the rent is cheap – less than I'm paying for B&B – the view over the river is glorious, and we can carry on saving a little for a deposit on a home of our own. And we'll be together.' He smiled happily.

Anthony couldn't see a downside. 'Congratulations anyway. I'm happy for you. I wish we could get word to Mum and Dad, and the girls.' He caught himself and shook his head. 'Forget it, we shouldn't be thinking about them. This is a new start, we have to forget home. *This* is home now.'

Tomas was suspiciously quiet, and Anthony cursed himself for spoiling the moment. 'Come on kid, cheer up...'

His brother shrugged. 'Do you think this was where Great-Grandma was born? Here? This farm?'

Anthony shook his head. 'We can't know. She didn't even remember herself, she was a kid, remember?'

Tomas cleared his throat, remembering the story. 'She said she came out of Lancashire, there were half a dozen kids, weren't there? She said they'd been sent away to hide, because there were rumours from Cornwall that the White Pack were back, and hunting us mongrels down.'

His brother put a steadying hand on his shoulder. 'The White Pack are busy in France, and Spain now. Their numbers are lower than they were back then. They sent hundreds of men to England and Wales a century ago. Now they send out a dozen, at most. Our older brothers and sisters didn't die cheaply.'

Tomas snorted. 'They breed as fast as we do

Fight for the Future

... faster, because they're not hiding and running. They'll come, one day. Like they did for those little kids. Great-Grandma had gone to get supplies, that's why she lived. How did they know? How did they know that those kids were werewolves?'

'She told Mum that one of the boys was in his wolf body when she found their bodies. He must have recognised the White Pack on the road, and perhaps he panicked, and tried to change, to protect the kids.'

'Stupid.' Tomas muttered. 'So stupid.'

'He was fourteen.' Anthony shuddered.

The brothers changed, and ran again, flushing out a confused pheasant and sharing it between them. They buried the feathers carefully. They returned to where they had left their clothes, and went their separate ways home.

The following evening, Tomas and Miriam visited the farm. Miriam was her usual chatty self, but looked tired and ill. Eddie heard the story, and flushed a deep angry red.

'Your dad has thrown you out?' he exclaimed. 'Where are you staying?'

Miriam blushed. 'In the pub, just until we're married and move into the flat. I've got a room, not with Tom, the landlady doesn't want to upset my dad too much.' Miriam's father was a local magistrate, with influence on the licensing committee.

Eddie went to the hall and picked up the phone.

'Jim? It's Eddie. Eddie Shepherd. I've got

your lass here. What the bloody hell do you think you're playing at?'

He listened for a moment.

'I'll say one thing, Jim. 1944. Do you get my drift?' He listened again, and then came back into the kitchen smiling dangerously.

'That was a card I'd hoped never to play. Miriam, he'll speak to the landlady – if you want to share Tomas's room, there'll be no repercussions for anyone. If you want to go back home and get your things, you can keep 'em here until you move into the flat. Alternatively, you can move in with us and share Frannie's room with her. Your dad is a good man, basically, but he forgets what it's like to be young. Fortunately for you, I remember what I was like ... and what he was like too.'

'1944?' said Miriam. 'Dad was in France, fighting. I was just a little girl.'

'Aye. It's his tale to tell though, not mine. But don't take any nonsense from him about this baby. Alreet?'

Miriam blushed deeply. 'I think I understand.'

'I'll stand witness. I'll give you away too, if you'd like? If old prune-face doesn't come round.'

Miriam shrugged. It did pretty things to her dark curls. 'I want him to be there. He and my brother are my only close relatives.'

The young couple left, and Eddie sighed, taking his seat in the armchair, staring at Anthony as if he was a new and interesting species of bug.

'Reet, lad. What have you got to say for

yourself?'

'I'm not Tomas,' Anthony said.

'Aye. And for that, I'm grateful.' The farmer relaxed, and Anthony went back to his cabin.

Chapter 13

The marriage was a low-key affair. Miriam defiantly wore a short white dress and matching jacket. Her father turned up at the last minute, and stood as her witness. Her brother didn't show at all. Anthony stood witness for Tomas. Both of the twins were nervous; it was the first real test of the false identities they had set up when they first arrived in England. The documents survived inspection, and Tomas took possession of the marriage certificate, sliding it into his inside pocket.

The six of them went straight to the Black Dog, where the landlady served a three course meal with cheap champagne in the small lounge, closing it to the public for a couple of hours. She refused payment and cried when Tomas left, with his new bride, to take up residence in the small flat above the chippy.

Eddie drove them back to the farm. 'We'll do a lot better than that for you two,' he said grimly. 'That poor lass. Queen of the village last year, she was. Now she's cramped into that tiny flat.'

Anthony spoke up. 'It won't be for long. Tomas will make sure of that.'

'Aye, mebbe.' He coughed. 'I hope that if you two aren't being good, you're being careful.'

Anthony closed his eyes. Frannie blushed. Neither of them spoke. Eddie cleared his throat again. 'Well, none of my business.'

Over the next few weeks, Frannie grew more distant

Fight for the Future

with Anthony, not seeking him out, avoiding him at mealtimes. He grew increasingly puzzled. Surely she couldn't be blaming him for Tomas's mistake…

One Sunday afternoon, coming home from chapel with her sisters, he took her arm. 'Frances. I want to talk to you. What's the matter?'

'I don't want to talk about it,' she said.

'I don't even know what you don't want to talk about,' he replied.

Frances slowed down, glaring at her fiancé until he let go of her arm.

'You and that brother of yours. You're so pleased about Miriam being pregnant.'

'She's quite happy about it too. Don't you want to be an auntie?'

'No. I don't want to be an auntie, or a grandmother, or a mother. Does that make it clear?' She looked away.

'Don't be daft,' Anthony said nervously.

'I'm not being daft. Look at me! I'm barely seven and a half stone with my shoes on. I get tired out kneading bread. My mother *died* a month after I was born. It was having me that killed her. I'm not fit to be a mother. I don't want to do it. We don't have to. We can be married without having children, can't we?'

Anthony was speechless. Frances stopped and he carried on, shaking his head. She waited for him to stop, and called out when he didn't. He turned and waited for her. When she caught up, he shook his head.

'No, Frannie. We can't. If it never happens, I can live with it. But we *have* to try. I want children. I dream about it, I dream about a son who looks like you. I won't argue about this, Frannie. If you won't change your mind, then we'll have to call it off.'

She was livid with shock. 'You don't love me,' she stated.

They looked at each other in despair. 'Frannie, I adore you. But this isn't an option for me.'

'You'd risk my life? For the chance of a child? Anthony, I can't believe this. Don't you know how strongly I feel?'

'I guess I do. It makes sense now, the way you won't let me anywhere near you. Now you're saying that you'll be the same when we get married?'

'No, there's a new pill out in America. There's a rumour that it will be available for married women next year in this country. I'll take that. It's very reliable. I thought if I took it, I could keep you happy ... that way.'

He let out a breath he hadn't known he was holding. 'You've gone to all this trouble to find out ways of not having a baby with me? Frances, you're making me feel sick with this. I can't deal with it.'

Maisie had noticed that they were hanging back, and stopped. Frannie waved to her to carry on without them, and turned her attention back to Anthony. 'Then I guess you'll have to decide what's more important to you,' she said simply.

Anthony wiped his eyes. She realised with a shock that he was in tears. 'Frannie...' he appealed.

She wiped her own eyes. 'No. I won't risk my

life. I want to do something with it. I don't want to die unloved and useless like my mother did.'

'Oh, that's not fair. That's not fair at all. Eddie loved your mum, in his own way. He did. Not like he loved Lily, but he cared about her. He misses her every day. I can tell.'

'He still let her die though.'

'I won't let you die,' Anthony said, with absolute conviction.

'No, you won't get the chance. If you can't accept this, we're finished.'

He looked at her, tears streaming down his face. 'I love you so much,' he said. Then he turned and walked back towards the village.

She watched him go, disbelief on her narrow face. She stood and watched him walk away from her, and when he was out of sight, she sat down at the side of the road. She drew her knees up, wrapped her arms around her legs, and sat staring into space. He didn't come back.

After half an hour, Eddie pulled up in the car. 'Tha'd best get in,' he said shortly. She did, staying quiet as he turned the car round and drove to the farm. At the gate he waited for her to jump out and open it, but she sat staring into space. Eddie took a deep breath and did it himself, driving through and getting out again to close it. When they got home, she got out of the car and went straight to Anthony's cabin. Eddie followed her in. She was lying on the bed, hugging the pillow.

'He doesn't love me,' she said dully.

'What's brought this on?'

'He wants us to have a baby.'

'What? Now?' Eddie was puzzled.

'No, one day. After we're married.' She managed a small smile. 'Dad, you can stop worrying about me. We've only kissed. Nothing more. It's crazy, I love him, but we've just kissed. Dad, I really do love him, but he doesn't want me, he doesn't love me.'

'Where is he?' Eddie sounded resigned.

'I don't know. He was walking towards the village.'

'Right, stay here. Don't do owt stupid.'

She lay on the bed, hugging the pillow, hearing the car start up again and drive away. Maisie popped her head around the door.

'Are you all right?'

'No.'

'Am I in charge then?'

'Yes. Go away, please.'

Her thirteen-year-old sister sighed and left. Frannie took things so seriously.

Eddie parked up outside the pub and went in, establishing that Anthony had enquired about his old room, but it was occupied. None of the other rooms were free, and he'd left.

Eddie's heart skipped a beat. He knew Anthony's reaction to rejection, and prayed that he could get to him before he disappeared again. He ran across town to the chippy, spotting his young farmhand sitting by the riverbank, skipping stones across the water.

He sat next to him 'You're still here.'

Fight for the Future

'No buses until tomorrow,' Anthony said simply.

'Don't go. I'll sort things out.'

'It's not something that can be sorted out. I want kids, she doesn't. We love each other. I don't want anyone else, she doesn't want anyone else, but we can't have a life together.'

Eddie took a deep breath. 'Look lad, I'll sort it. She's being stubborn because she thinks tha'll come round. She doesn't understand what you are.'

Anthony stiffened. 'What do you mean by that?' he said. There was a dangerous edge to his voice that made Eddie shiver. He was uncomfortably aware that he was in a quiet place with a strong young man who was in a very unpredictable mood.

Eddie sighed. 'Tha's been clever. But tha you don't understand how long legends last in a place like this. Ah'm a bit of a student of local history, like mi grandad before me. And Ah'm a farmer too, Ah understand bloodlines. In fact, if we compare notes, I think tha'll find we've both got a lot of information about several bloodlines whose ancestors disappeared a few generations back, leaving some of their kids behind.'

Anthony kept his voice light, casual. 'I don't know what you're talking about, Eddie.'

'Don't lie to me. Ah know thee too well. Tha's, a werewolf.' As he said it, he disbelieved it – that he was sitting by the riverbank, speaking to a dark foreigner about legends and nightmares.

Anthony sighed, avoiding the question. 'I want her. Eddie, I know she's your daughter, but I want her so bloody much. She's a bad-tempered, stubborn little madam, and I want to spend my life with her.'

Eddie shook his head, heartbroken for them. 'That's just it though, isn't it? Tha could live for a century, mebbe more, if t'legends are true. And from what Ah've seen, she'll be lucky to hit sixty.'

The young shapeshifter shivered, and then whispered. 'How did you know?'

'Ah.' The farmer sighed. It was an admission. 'So you are?'

Anthony looked around. They were unobserved. His eyes took on a look of deep concentration, and Eddie stared in fascination as Anthony's left forearm shortened, the fingers turning outwards, growing claws, fur. For three seconds, he was looking at a wolf's foreleg, grafted horribly to a human body. He shuddered. Anthony relaxed, and his arm returned to normal.

'Does that answer your question? How did you guess? Where did I go wrong?'

'Ah well, Ah know t' legends, and Ah like to think Ah'm open-minded. The first thing was a pair of identical twins turning up and trying to settle down here, of all places. Two good-looking lads come all the way from southern France and decide that a little village in the middle of nowhere is where they want to make their home? Come on!'

Anthony looked around at the heaven he had found. 'You'd be surprised. But carry on.'

'Well, you arrived, and t' first thing you did was start gossiping wi' t'old men. Only when you'd had chance to work out bloodlines did you start courting. And you courted with absolute single-mindedness. Miriam was t'obvious choice. But she was already engaged. The two of you cut her away from Jennison like wolves cutting a lamb from its mother.'

Anthony laughed at the comparison. 'Miriam's no lamb,' he commented.

'No, wrong metaphor. But you worked together, Ah watched you. It was impressive. Subtle, clever, and absolutely masterful. How did tha decide who got her?'

The younger man lay back, shielding his eyes from the sun. 'Her choice. I reckon she got it right.'

Eddie nodded. 'Then once Miriam was with Tomas, tha moved in on Linda. That ended suddenly. Ah were very suspicious by then. There's half a dozen lasses round here who are younger, prettier, and more fun than Linda, but they didn't exist as far as you were concerned. Ah tried to warn you that she wasn't what tha wanted. Ah told you she was good stock.'

'Yes. I remember. So you suspected what was going on when you told me about Frannie's mum?'

'Yes. And Ah thought, who better to take care of my frail little lass, to love her, than someone like you? Someone strong, who would treasure her. She deserved better than the oafs she was meeting in the cafe. Ah worried that Ah might be being callous to her, that you'd like as not give her a safe marriage but nowt else. It worked out better than Ah'd hoped, didn't it? And there were other things too.'

'What?'

'The first night you stayed, the rats disappeared. That young tomcat's keen, but he's not that good. Tha should have been a bit more subtle.'

'Maybe.' Anthony shrugged.

'T'foxes are scared of the henhouse,' Eddie said.

'Ah.'

'And last, but not least, Vinnie Travers had an odd tale to tell about a big rabid dog attacking him the same night tha got rid of the rest of the vermin. It all adds up, if tha knows where to look.'

Anthony sighed. 'I guess it's time to move on. And tell Tomas what you know.'

Eddie rolled his eyes. 'Ah've kept quiet til now. I can keep quiet until the day Ah die. You're a man, same as me. Aren't you? Just a man with some odd talents. Ah like you, Ah trust you, and you're a damn good worker. Look, take t'car will you? Those terrier pups are ready now. I paid the woman to keep 'em with their mum an extra week or two, they're fine little things. T'address is on this bit of paper. Ah was going to go for them today anyway. Ah'll walk back, and sort things with Frances. You get the puppies, come back, and talk to her again. If it doesn't work out, tha can leave tomorrow, but at least pick up your money and clothes, eh?'

'We'll see,' said Anthony. 'You have to keep this secret though. I can't tell you how important it is.'

'Ah won't tell a soul. Ah guess there's a reason why you're hiding here, and I won't tell tha secret. If tha want Frances to know, tha can tell her yourself.'

'If I tell her, she'll never believe that I love her for herself, not for the potential that she carries. I never want her to doubt me.'

The men walked back to the pub, and Anthony drove away towards Carnforth. Eddie walked home.

The door to the cabin was open, and Eddie walked in. Frannie was lying on the bed, staring at the ceiling. She was holding a scrap of paper. She held it out to her father. He looked at it and smiled. It was a pretty sketch of Frannie, wearing her red party dress, barefoot, her hair long and loose, her expression bright and challenging. 'I found this under the pillow. I didn't know he could draw,' she said. Eddie held the paper up to the light; there were signs of many changes.

'He took a long time getting this right, you know?'

'So what?' Frannie was defensive now.

Eddie took her hand. 'Frances. He won't change his mind on this. Tha can wrap him around your little finger for t' rest of your life, just like you've been doing for the last few months. But this is t'sticking point. Ah've talked to him, and he's not bluffing. The lad adores you but if you don't back down on this, it will be the biggest mistake of your life.'

'I can't have kids. You know I'm not strong enough. Mum died!'

'Dottie died because Ah was a bad husband.

Ah was a teenage dad. Ah'd lost my grandad and both parents in the space of two years. Ah had a farm to run, a sick wife and an ailing baby. Ah was still grieving for my family, and couldn't cope. She needed rest and love and reassurance, and got none of it. She didn't *want* to live. My fault. Anthony will look after you, support you, love you. Not only that, Dottie died over seventeen years ago. Childbirth is a lot safer now. Frances, for my sake, don't let how Ah failed your mother stop *you* from finding happiness. It would be another punishment on me. If Ah thought this would kill you, does that really think I'd be saying this?'

'No,' she whispered.

'Will tha tell him he gets what he wants on this?'

'Yes,' she said in a small voice, turning away and hugging the pillow to her.

An hour later, she heard the car draw up. She heard her sisters crowd around, laughing and cooing with delight as Anthony handed puppies to the three eldest. She heard her father come out and order everyone indoors, making blustering comments about how the pups weren't to be spoiled, they were ratters, not pets. She heard Anthony's soft, even steps across the yard, and sat upright, smoothing the pillow out, sitting on the edge of the bed.

He pushed the door open wearily.

'I'm sorry,' she said. 'Dad's spoken to me, made me see things differently. Of course we can try to have a baby. It's just a shock, talking about it like that. I'm only seventeen, I still feel like a kid myself.'

He sighed with relief. 'Hey, we can have fun first, some time alone. I just want to know that one day we'll have kids.'

'Plural?' she asked, appalled again.

Anthony smiled. 'Well, we'll see, eh? You might want more when you see how beautiful our babies can be.' He sat next to her, picking up the picture, looking at her.

'I'm not that pretty, really,' she said.

'No, of course you're not. I drew a picture of someone completely different because I love you so much,' he said blandly. His reward was her smile.

'Can we cuddle?' she said, suddenly. 'I mean, just cuddle, nothing else.'

'Frannie,' he sighed, lying down and drawing her to him. For the first time he felt her lying against him, body to body, her head nestled to his chest. Her hand reached up to his face, caressing his cheek, tentatively following the line of his tears to his eye, gently smoothing the wetness away.

'Don't cry, my love. It's going to be all right,' she said helplessly. 'Don't cry, I'm sorry. I'd do anything to make you happy.'

'I won't hurt you,' he said hoarsely. 'I never want to hurt you again. I never want to walk away from you again.'

They lay together, wrapped in each other's arms, until sleep came. Frannie woke up late at night, hungry and thirsty, and woke him gently. She kissed him, allowing herself to touch his thick glossy curls, to explore the sweet curve of his jawline. She sighed and drew away.

'I still want to wait, until we're married.'

'Me too,' he said. 'But can we get married tomorrow?'

She left.

Chapter 14

Anthony awoke to the din of rain on the roof of the shed. He checked the time: five o'clock. He'd slept for hours, and was ready to get up and start the chores. The cows first, then the chickens, then he'd think about getting some breakfast. He stretched, ready for the day. It had been a while since he'd slept for so long, but the events of yesterday had exhausted him.

An hour later, as he dumped the waste from the chicken coop on the manure heap, the kitchen door opened and Eddie peered out. 'Come in, you're getting soaked,' the older man hissed. 'You'll catch your death.'

Anthony didn't argue. The kitchen was already warm, and he pulled a chair up to the stove. 'Feels like summer is over...' he said.

'Aye, it might surprise us yet though.' Eddie bit his lip. 'How's things with Frannie?' He was keeping his voice low.

'We're fine, I think.' The farmhand shrugged, and changed the subject. 'Where are the pups?'

'In wi' Maisie and Susan. On the bed. Ah've told 'em but...' It was Eddie's turn to shrug. 'We'll separate 'em to train 'em, or we'll end up with a bloody pack.' He took a long look at Anthony, then stood up and went to the counter, pouring a pint of tea from the big teapot, adding a drop of milk, and handing it to Anthony. 'Speaking of packs ... isn't that what you call your families?'

Anthony shrugged. 'Families, we usually call

them families. But ... well, we call the others 'Pack'. He swallowed, wondering if this was something he could talk about with Eddie.

'Others?' Eddie blinked. 'The ones that killed the Vernes?'

'Vernes?' Anthony looked puzzled.

'The ones who had this farm before it was the Shepherd farm. The werewolves. Mi grandad told me about them. Tha said tha were descended from them...' Eddie frowned. 'Didn't tha?'

'I didn't know they had this farm.' Anthony swallowed. 'Bloody hell. I never knew that.' He looked round. 'The farmhouse...'

'Not the same one, we built this a hundred years ago.'

'After my great-gran escaped.' Anthony nodded. 'She wasn't called Verne. There were other names than hers, other families. I can't remember all the stories, or the names. The people who killed her family, and the other families, we call them the White Pack. We ... me and Tomas, we're hiding out here. They won't come back, we hope.'

'And what's the quarrel? Ah know they came here and killed dozens of people...'

'Hundreds, the stories say.' Anthony shuddered. 'One farm at a time. Took 'em all night. They were expected, the farms were defended, but there were so many of them, and they were so vicious. As for why ... well, look at *human* history. Genocide isn't that rare. They don't like us. They think we're scum, impure, heretics.'

'Why do they think that?' Eddie was old

enough to know that there were two sides to every tale.

Anthony stared at him. 'Religion. Their religion. It's messed up. They think they should keep to themselves. It's not always been like that, even a hundred years ago there were White Pack men, even some women, who would leave their home and find their fortune in the world. Every werewolf in Europe is descended from the Whites, ultimately. My dad's grandma was a half-blood, born to an Austrian lass and a White Pack trader who settled down away from the Pack.'

He took a deep drink of the tea. 'Is it too early for something stronger?' he joked. He glanced at the stairs.

Eddie understood, he shook his head. 'They'll be asleep for a while yet. We've got a few minutes to talk. Why did things change?'

'God knows. I don't. New leaders? I don't know ... I know that the First ... their chief, sort of, he's very religious. His father was too. They've taken power away from the women, from what I've heard.' Anthony managed a smile. 'In case you didn't know, we do tend to defer to our women.'

'Aye, that's why you feel at home round here, no doubt.' Eddie returned the smile.

'That'll be it. Anyway, over the last century or so, they've got stricter and stricter, so we've heard. Nobody leaves. They've stopped taking wives and husbands from outside the Pack. They're becoming increasingly inbred, but it doesn't seem to hurt them. They're strong, fit, and they're bloody angry with us.'

His voice trembled. 'They say we abandon our babies!'

Eddie scowled. 'And?'

'Sometimes, we have to. The Whites, they look for us. They look for families with twins. They look for families with a lot of kids. When there were lots of us, we swapped twins with each other, to stay under the radar. As our numbers shrank, we had to leave them in orphanages. Tom and I left home at fourteen, because we have...' He fell silent. 'Sorry Eddie, the less you know, the better.'

'Why did tha leave home? What made tha so scared?'

'Mama made us leave.' Anthony stood up. 'Look, the girls will be awake soon. I'm going to check the stream. I noticed a tree branch ready to drop yesterday and this rain ... I don't want the stream to flood ...'

'Did someone die?' Eddie was relentless.

'Stop it, Eddie.' Anthony wiped his face.

'Ah need to know.'

'Lots of us died. One by one. Sisters, brothers. By the time I was born, that's all there was, our little family, no cousins, they'd all been hunted down. My parents were the last of their family, they're cousins to each other. They had no choice of mate. We stopped trying to visit each other, because we never knew who was following, who was keeping track. Now, are you satisfied? Because you know too much.'

'Will they look for thee here?' Eddie asked, so quietly it was almost a whisper.

'I hope not. We ran a long way to get away. They think they've wiped us out in England.' Anthony looked long and hard into Eddie's eyes. 'I hope not.'

Chapter 15

Anthony sat in the warm farmhouse kitchen, nursing his guitar, haltingly picking out the tune for 'It's Now or Never'. He'd been listening alternately to the Ben E King and Elvis recordings, and had the basics. Eddie was napping in the armchair, catching sleep when he could get it. Outside the rain poured down, and strong winds lashed the farm. Anthony was itching to get in the car and intercept Frannie on her way home from work, but he knew he would get scant thanks if he did.

He pricked up his ears as he heard the garden gate open, but no corresponding clang as it shut again. He stood up warily. Frannie always shut the gate after her. Before he could get to the door, it flew open and Frannie ran in, soaked through and dishevelled.

'Anthony, we've got to get to the hospital, it's Miriam.'

Eddie woke up as the cold March air hit the kitchen. He blinked, seeing Frannie scared and wet through. 'What's going on?'

'Miriam, she's been taken to the cottage hospital, it's the baby,' Frannie said impatiently. 'Give Anthony the car keys ... please. Please, everyone says that Tomas is going mad. They said at the pub they were going to ring you!'

Eddie struggled to his feet and started to look for the keys. Anthony went to put his shoes on.

'Frannie, get changed, honey. We can spare five minutes for you to get into some dry clothes.'

Fight for the Future

'No, Tomas is going mad.'

'In that case, there's no time for you to stand arguing, is there? I don't want you ill too. You should get changed quickly.'

She opened her mouth to argue, but then turned and ran upstairs. Anthony walked out to the hall. He picked up the phone, listened for a moment, and then went back into the kitchen.

'The line is down. It must be those winds. What are we going to do about the girls?'

Eddie dismissed his worries. 'They love this weather, the lot of them, mad kiddies. They'll get home wet through and laughing their heads off. Tough little beggars, like Lily. Ah'll get the fire stoked up and the stove hot. You see to tha brother.'

Frannie came running downstairs in dry clothes and her summer shoes. Anthony looked at her thin shoes and frowned. As they got to the kitchen door he looked at the inch deep rainwater bouncing in the farmyard, and scooped her off her feet. 'We won't get your feet wet,' he explained hurriedly, carrying her through the gate to the car and opening the door.

She was still spluttering at him when he sat beside her and started the engine, giving it maximum choke. It started first time, and he eased the car down the lane, which was now a fast-flowing shallow stream.

'Where is the hospital?' he asked quietly.

'Go through the village, take the next left, through Mickledale and it's about three miles up the road.' Frannie was beginning to tremble with delayed shock. Anthony reached behind him and took a blanket from the back seat. Frannie accepted it wordlessly, and drew it up around herself. He put the heater on full.

He was silent for a while, negotiating the narrow single-track lane through a sudden squall of heavy hail. When he reached the road he switched the lights on, and headed for the village. The driving conditions eased, and he spoke again.

'Tell me what you know,' he said quietly.

Frannie collected her thoughts. 'I was at work. We weren't busy, not many customers in this weather. I was cleaning the ovens when Molly Dawson from the chippy came running into the pub. She said Miriam had been taken badly, and rang for the ambulance. I ran over to see Tom and Miriam, and she was unconscious. Tom wouldn't be parted from her, and he went with her in the ambulance when it came.' She was quiet for a moment, then blurted out, 'There was a lot of blood, Anthony. I'm scared.'

'I understand. We'll be with them soon, we'll find out everything.'

They drove in silence until they got to the hospital. It wasn't much to look at, just two or three wards, and a small casualty department. They parked close to the entrance and ran in. The receptionist looked up. 'Mr Preston? Anthony Preston?'

He nodded.

'Your brother and his wife are in a side room. I'll take you to them. Is this your sister?'

'My fiancée,' he said. The nurse looked at the

powerfully built young man. His skinny girlfriend looked about fourteen years old, she had mud on her face, and was wearing an old coat that was three sizes too big for her. She sighed. Some farm boys had no sense, but it was none of her business. Frannie saw the look and interpreted it correctly.

'You can take that expression off your face right now. I'm nearly eighteen, we're getting married later this year, and he's a perfect gentleman.'

Anthony looked at her, puzzled. The receptionist blushed, but escorted them to a small, dark room where Miriam lay sleeping in a narrow bed, encased in starched sheets and uncomfortable-looking woollen blankets. Tomas sat next to her, the colour was drained from his features. Every few minutes, he'd reach out to touch her forehead, then pull back nervously. He looked up, relief on his face when he saw his twin.

He tried to stand up, but Anthony was with him quickly, kneeling on the floor next to him and taking him in his arms, holding him close. Nobody spoke. The receptionist left. Frannie moved to the other side of the bed and sat down, watching Miriam's steady breathing.

She waited until the brothers had broken their embrace, then spoke. 'What happened?'

Tomas shut his eyes tightly, then spoke quickly. 'Something went wrong. The baby came too soon. She died before she was born.'

'She?' asked Anthony.

'Yes, they said it was a girl. We were going to name her Johanna, if she was a girl.' Tomas looked bewildered, still caught in a world where he and his bride were collecting baby clothes and planning names. He looked at Anthony. 'We didn't see her. They said they would deal with everything for us.'

'Huh,' said Frannie very quietly, and Anthony turned to her.

'What does that mean?' he asked her.

She shook her head. 'It depends on whether they see her as a baby or not.'

Tomas shuddered. 'She's my daughter. She was kicking last night when I sang to her.'

Anthony was already out of the room. He sensed that time was critical. He strode through the building, ignoring protests, until he came to the small morgue. There was only one body there, a heartbreakingly tiny form on a cold stainless steel table, an array of instruments set out next to her. A masked form spun round, and muttered angrily, 'You can't come in here.'

Anthony stood between the small corpse and the medic. 'What are you going to do to my niece?' he asked mildly.

'Your niece?'

'The baby girl,' he explained. The medic's eyes widened.

'Your niece? We need to know why she died. I was going to do a post-mortem.'

'Is it necessary? Legally?'

'Not exactly, but the parents may want answers.'

'What will you do with her afterwards?' Anthony was still calm. He could see the sense in

Fight for the Future

what he had been told.

'She'll be buried quietly next time a grave is opened for another burial. Most parents don't want a funeral for a stillborn premature birth.'

'Johanna will have a funeral,' said Anthony. 'And I will stay here to make sure that you treat her with respect. When you've finished, I'm taking her back to her mother and father. Do you understand?'

The medic nodded. He understood perfectly. He'd always felt uncomfortable about this aspect of the job. He started to cut into the tiny body, keeping an eye on the man, convinced that he would faint. He didn't, but moved closer, inspecting the work. When the internal organs had been examined and notes had been taken, the medic took a small saw and moved to her head. Anthony coughed, and he stopped.

'I'm not telling you how to do your job, but could you let me know what you've found out so far?'

'Well, the foetus—'

'Johanna,' insisted Anthony.

'Johanna was underdeveloped for her age. Her internal organs weren't developing. Her heart was faulty, and that's probably what killed her. She was dead before her mother went into labour.'

'So what are you going to do now?'

'I was going to look at her brain.'

'No, we have our answers. It's enough. I can dress her, hide what you've done to her body. But you won't touch her face. She's beautiful, and her mother deserves to see that. Do you sew her up now?'

'Yes. I hope you don't mind, but I have to say

that you're very composed. Do you have medical training?'

'No, but I've seen death before. And shouting and screaming wouldn't have helped either of us, would it?'

The medic was about to thank him, and then realised that Anthony's 'us' embraced uncle and niece, not the medic himself. He nodded. 'I think the nurses keep some doll's clothes for premmies. If you ask at the nurses' common room, they'll find something pretty for Johanna. I'll sew her up and clean her.'

As Anthony left the room, the medic bent to his task, suddenly aware that the tiny body had been transformed from the object of a routine procedure into 'Johanna'. He sighed, cradling her as he took her to the sink, and began to bathe the cold little body. He wrapped her in a clean towel, and laid her back on the table.

When her uncle returned, they dressed her together in a pink knitted dress and bonnet. Anthony nodded his thanks, and carried her back to her parents.

Tomas rose to his feet, his hands open in front of him to receive his daughter. 'Why?' he asked.

'It was the child, not Miriam. Johanna wouldn't have lived. She's been opened up so we could know why she died. Her heart was wrong, Tomas. I've told the hospital that we're going to take her home. You and Miriam have to decide where she will be buried.'

'She's so cold. It's not been that long, surely?'

said Tomas.

'She was probably dead for a while before she was born,' explained Anthony. He looked at Frannie. 'Are you going to be all right?'

Frances was stiff-faced. 'I'll be fine. It's life, isn't it? It's unfair, she was wanted so much, even if she wasn't intended.'

Anthony glanced at his brother. Frances's tactlessness was becoming legendary, but Tomas ignored it. He drew Anthony out of the room.

'She wasn't like us?' he whispered.

Anthony shook his head. 'We just don't have enough information about this kind of pregnancy. Whatever Miriam is, whether she carries the trait or not, we still don't know. We might never know.'

'She's alive, that's the important thing. I'm staying off work for a while, until she's better.'

Frannie came out. 'I'll speak to Dad. You two can stay at the farm if you want, that flat isn't suitable for Miriam until she's well. There's no proper bathroom for a start. You can have my room. I'll bunk in with Maisie and Susan for a few weeks.'

Tomas's pride warred with common sense for a while, and love won. 'Thank you, Frances. When she's well enough to leave here, I'll bring her to the farm. Are you sure your father will be OK?'

'He'd better be,' said Frannie grimly.

There was a noise behind them, and Miriam was awake. She was still heavily sedated, and peered through the open doorway at Tomas. 'Wha...' she managed. He walked back to her, picking their daughter up from the foot of the bed, and looking at Miriam, wondering how he was going to tell her.

Chapter 16

In the cool early hours, the twins sat on the farm gate, staring at the moon.

'Fancy a run?' asked Tomas, listlessly.

'I don't have the energy. I just want to sleep. What about you?'

'Me too. Divvy up, eh?'

Anthony reached into his pocket and took out a wad of fivers. Tomas's eyes widened. 'How much?'

'Fifty. Twenty for tonight, and three tenners as deposit for gigs next month. We had two last-minute cancellations last month, and we can't afford to lose money like that. From now on we ask for a deposit.'

'Great. Twenty-five quid! That's magic. I think we've gone as high as we can though...'

Anthony was smiling too. 'How's the deal going with Alf?'

Alf was the builder who was building a small private estate of semi-detatched houses at the edge of the village. Tomas was negotiating heavily with him. He winked.

'Ten per cent discount for me, if me and my boss do the plumbing in two of the houses for free. I've spoken to my boss, and he says it's my wedding present, late. And that I'm doing unpaid overtime for the next month.'

Anthony laughed. Everyone won, except the taxman. 'Did you ask him about me too?'

'Yeah, he's offered a five per cent discount,

he needs another labourer for a month. I explained that you had a job, and he says you can fit it around.'

Anthony shrugged. He was a fast worker, and strong, and the only thing to suffer would be his time with Frannie, and practice time on his guitar. For a month's hard work, he'd be spared a nice chunk of debt. He fingered the cash in his pocket. Things were going well. Eddie had accepted that they were moving out after the wedding, and had begun training Maisie to take over the morning milking.

'Well then, I'll see you on Tuesday, eh? Frannie and I will come over to visit. How is Miriam?'

'She's coping. Physically she's fine. That fortnight at the farm got her back on her feet, but she just broods all the time. The doctor says she needs another baby to think about, but we know that might be easier said than done.' Tomas looked frustrated. He bit his lip. 'Johanna would be here by now, if she'd lived.'

Anthony slid off the gate, and looked at his twin. 'Johanna's in the past.' He thought back briefly to the rainy afternoon in the muddy graveyard of the chapel. He and Tomas had made the coffin between them, and Frannie had made a lining for it out of scraps of white material that Miriam had handed to her. She'd only realised halfway through the work that it was Miriam's wedding dress. The baby had a headstone and a grave, and Miriam had a place to sit and mourn.

The twins hugged briefly, then Tomas hauled his pushbike from where he'd stashed it earlier behind the gate, and Anthony drove back to the farm. He glanced up at Frannie's window, and was happy to see the curtains open a little. She stood and waved, and then the light went out. He looked around the farmyard. All was well. He fell into his cabin, and went to sleep with his clothes still on.

Chapter 17

'Anthony dear, it's seven o'clock. Are you getting up?'

Mrs Martin stood nervously at the door. The party in the pub the previous night had ended in a lock-in, and her husband had been left to drag the groom upstairs. Tomas had been the last to leave, staggering home to the chippy muttering darkly about 'proper weddings'. Eddie had been taken home in a taxi at midnight, three hours after his usual bedtime. He'd last been heard comparing the charms of the local widows and older unmarried ladies, to hair-curling effect.

The landlady knocked on the door again. Her husband was sleeping it off still. They'd offered to host the party and give Anthony a free room for the night. The extra takings had more than compensated them for their generosity, as expected. She heard a muffled groan from inside the room.

'Anthony, you *have* to get up,' she hissed. 'You're getting married this afternoon. You need a good breakfast inside you.'

The door flew open, and she stepped aside just in time to see him run down the corridor to the bathroom, his hand clamped over his mouth. He was still wearing the jeans he'd been wearing last night. She closed her eyes patiently, giving him some privacy. She knocked on the bathroom door.

'Anthony. I've run you a bath. You don't have to use that old shower. You can use the family bathroom this morning.'

Fight for the Future

'Thanks,' he called, weakly, and then started to retch again.

'Men,' she muttered.

Half an hour later he was downstairs, dressed in pyjamas, smiling broadly, waiting expectantly for his breakfast.

'Well, you recovered quickly,' she commented. 'How many eggs?'

'How many have you got?' he asked, and she hit him fondly with her tea towel.

'You cheeky wretch. Eh lad, I remember the day you and Tom turned up here, you were a right pair of gypsies. I can't believe it was only last year. It feels like the two of you have always been here.'

Anthony was pleased. 'Thank you. Is that good?'

'Well, most people think so. I'll get your breakfast then.'

Anthony ate ravenously, and then went back upstairs to rest and play his guitar. At ten, Tomas arrived. He was a little pale, but calm. He adopted a 'been there, done that' air, much to his brother's amusement.

'Tomas, stop being superior, and tell me that you've not lost the ring.'

His twin made a show of patting his pockets, first absentmindedly and then worriedly.

'Whoops,' he said mournfully.

'You bastard. Stop messing about.'

'Enjoy your bad language, you'll have to stop it at two o'clock today.'

'Yeah? Give me the bloody ring, Tomas. I'll

look after it myself until we get to the chapel.'

Tomas sniffed theatrically. 'Unbeliever. Trust me.'

Anthony grabbed hold of him and wrestled him to the ground, laughing as he did so. 'You bugger. Don't mess with me. Submit or be thrashed.'

Tomas's eyes flashed once, that strange silver fire that was reflected in his twin's pupils. He relaxed. 'I miss you,' he said quietly. 'I love Miriam, but I miss you. It will be nice living next door to each other.'

His brother relaxed, standing up. 'Yeah, it will be good. We'll see more of each other, I hope. Maybe Miriam and Frannie will even be friends.'

Tomas nodded. The two women were polite to each other, and had genuinely tried to find common ground, but they were just too different from each other to form any true bond of friendship. He sat on the bed. 'Well, everyone else seems to be running this wedding. What shall we do for the next few hours? It will only take a few minutes for us to get dressed.'

Anthony reached under the bed and pulled out his guitar. He smiled. 'Nobody's going to tell me to keep quiet today, I guess. Go get yours, we'll practise. It will be odd tonight, being at a wedding and not playing.' He sighed. Frannie had insisted on having a folk band play, and he'd spent the last fortnight learning the dance steps to half a dozen pieces of music.

They spent the morning playing songs, new and old, and by the afternoon were gently playing folk music that they remembered from their childhood. They talked quietly about their parents and siblings, and their hopes for the future. An hour before the ceremony, they dressed in their new suits, checked once more that the ring was safe, and walked slowly to the chapel.

It was set back a little, on the road out of the village. Halfway up a small hill, it had a pleasant well-kept garden at the front, and a small graveyard at the back. It was a simple brick building with double wooden doors. There was a small group waiting already. Anthony stopped in sudden terror. 'I can't believe I'm doing this,' he whispered.

'Frannie. It's just Frannie,' Tomas told him. 'Just your girl, relax, it's going to be fine. If you want, I'll do it for you?'

Anthony giggled nervously. 'Frannie can tell us apart.'

'Sure she can.' Tomas winked, and Anthony's eyes widened until he realised that Tomas just had to be winding him up. He shook his head, and approached the guests.

Most of them were relatives of Frannie's on her dad's side. Lily and Dottie had very few living relatives. Frannie's aunts and uncles were surrounded by about a dozen children. Six of them, dressed in frightening amounts of pink lace and net, were Frannie's sisters. She'd explained that she couldn't choose between them for a bridesmaid, so they would all have to do it. Standing to one side, her hair adorned with a pretty arrangement of flowers, wearing a pale pink dress, was Miriam, the matron of honour. She was glowing with pleasure. Anthony watched as Tomas's facial expression darkened for a moment. He and Miriam had never had this summer moment. The sun shone on her dark, loose curls, and Tomas glanced back at his twin, who was suddenly chatting politely to Mr and Mrs Martin. He walked up to his wife, standing behind her, putting his arms around her, and kissing her neck gently. She stiffened, then relaxed.

'You look pretty,' he told her.

'So do you,' she said, gently mocking him.

'I want you,' he whispered. She closed her eyes. He'd barely touched her since they'd lost Johanna. 'Thank God for that,' she sighed, leaning back against him. 'I thought...'

'Well, stop thinking. Just let's pretend that tonight is our wedding night too. It's been too long.'

'Damn right,' she whispered. She suddenly realised they were being watched, and smiled wickedly, turning around in his embrace, kissing him with a suddenly remembered passion, letting her hands rest on his hips. She relished the hissed intake of breath from some of the watching guests.

She broke away, laughing. 'OK, handsome, let's break it up for now. We don't want to steal the kid's thunder, do we? Come on, we'd better get inside, she'll be here soon.'

Tomas remembered that he had duties, and marshalled the six pink, lacy sisters into the chapel entrance, guided the rest of the guests to their seats, and made reassuring noises to Anthony, making him sit quietly at the front of the chapel. He went to the door. His wife was standing outside, waving to a car that was just pulling up. Tomas nodded. 'I'll leave you to it,' he said.

He strode down the aisle, and leaned over to his twin. 'They're here. Stand up. Don't wobble.'

Anthony stood silently at the front of the chapel, not daring to turn his head as the 'Wedding March' played. He could hear the congregation making faint noises of approval as the bride, her father, Miriam, and the pink cloud of bridesmaids made their way down the aisle. He glanced to the side as Frances took her place beside him. He could see nothing but an ivory blur; she wore a headdress with a tiny veil that just covered her face. He swallowed nervously. The vicar appeared, and the next half-hour passed in a blur of readings, hymns and dazedly exchanged vows of fidelity before he was guided into place for a seemingly endless set of photographs. Eventually, he was ushered into a car with Frances, and the door closed on them. As the driver pulled away to the reception venue, Anthony took the chance to look at her for the first time.

'Well?' she demanded.

'Very' he whispered. Her dress was tightly fitted in the body and arms, with what looked like several dozen layers of net in the skirt. Her hair was elaborately dressed, and her headdress was a simple white comb, holding the short veil in place.

He needed reassurance. 'Are you happy? Was it what you wanted?'

'Perfect, absolutely perfect. Right down to the stunned-looking groom.'

He turned and took her in his arms, kissing

her hard, almost desperately.

The driver called out. 'Oi! There's a meal yet, and a dance. Put her down.'

Anthony ignored him, only stopping when Frances pushed him back, laughing. 'Hey, I made a lot of promises back there, but giving up breathing wasn't one of them. Back off!'

'For now,' he whispered.

The day and the evening went by in a daze. People kept handing Anthony drinks, and Tomas kept taking them off him and replacing them with lemonade or Coke. He danced with every woman present, including his six new sisters-in-law. The youngest, Marian, was only four years old, and insisted on standing on his feet while he danced.

Eventually, he felt a small hand take hold of his, and he looked round. Frances had slipped away to get changed. She was wearing a deep crimson two-piece suit. It was a perfect fit for her, and he dizzily realised that she wasn't wearing anything but underwear beneath the jacket. 'You didn't break my rule,' he said, smiling at her, loving her.

'No? That's good. Now, the car is here. The bags are packed. Come with me.'

He looked around, so many people to say farewell to, but she shook her head. 'I've done all that. Just come with me.'

Tomas and Miriam were outside, leaning against the wall, kissing enthusiastically. They broke off to say hasty goodbyes to the newly-weds, and then went back indoors to supervise the party and make sure everyone was having fun.

Fight for the Future

It took only twenty minutes to get to the hotel where they were spending their wedding night, and the night porter took their bags to the room, palming the tip that Anthony gave him, and leaving unnervingly quickly. Anthony looked around, opening a door and marvelling at the cleanliness and size of the en-suite bathroom.

He looked at his bride. Frances was standing by the window, looking out over the hotel gardens. She was trembling, just a little, just enough for him to notice.

He coughed, and she turned slightly, her eyes wide. He smiled reassuringly. 'Do you want to use the bathroom?'

'No. I'm OK.' Her voice was firm. She was so good at controlling her voice, she sounded so adult, so confident. He managed not to grin. 'I'll have a quick shower then. I won't be too long.' He waited until she nodded and turned back to the window, and then he took his suit and shoes off and went into the bathroom. He stripped off and showered quickly, grabbed a thick white towel from the rack, and stood at the bathroom door, looking into the bedroom, unseen by Frances. She was barefoot, barelegged, her shoes placed neatly by the wardrobe, next to his, her stockings still in her hand. She was looking in the mirror, and she didn't seem happy with what she saw.

He wanted to go to her then, to tell her that she was exquisite, beautiful, his ... but something stopped him, some wicked desire to watch her when she thought she was unobserved. He knew that he might never see her in this way again, and he clung to each precious moment as he watched her undress, watched her smooth her suit and hang it carefully in the wardrobe. His weight shifted, and a board creaked under his foot. She looked up, towards the bathroom, and he ran back to the shower, turning it off, throwing the towel over his head and entering the bedroom, an expression of total innocence on his face.

He dropped the towel to the floor next to the bed, and looked up, smiling. His smile changed as he looked at her, becoming distracted. She stood there, slight and pale. He looked at her with pleasure, suddenly ecstatic that they'd waited until this night, that he could make love to her here, where it would be perfect.

In three short steps he was with her, his arms around her, kissing her hair, reaching for the clips that held it up, releasing it in a sudden dark wave around her white shoulders. He pulled her close. She shivered. He drew away and looked at her.

'Frannie? I won't hurt you.' He realised that her trembling was fear, not excitement, and he moved away, baffled. 'Sweetheart, I know it's your first time. Can't you trust me to love you? We've got all night,' he whispered. 'We've got so much to find out about each other.'

This time her shudder wasn't all fear, and the kiss that he whispered on her neck was echoed by a sudden crop of goose pimples.

He moved to the bed, pushing the sheet and quilt aside, reaching out to her.

'Frannie, come to me.'

Fight for the Future

She took an uncertain step towards the bed. Then, with the air of someone committing themselves to the void, she climbed in and lay next to him, unmoving.

'Anthony, I don't know. I really don't know. I don't talk about this. I don't know anything. Nobody tells me things, they just assume I *know*.'

'Like the bread?' he asked.

Her eyes opened in surprise. 'Yes, like the bread.' She smiled at him. 'That was good, the bread.'

'This can be better,' he whispered. 'Trust me?'

'If I say stop...?'

'I'll stop.'

But she didn't say stop for a long time, not until they'd learned so much more about each other, and not before his lips and tongue and his clever hands had brought her to a shuddering, giggling rush. 'Why did you make me wait until we were married for that?' she laughed.

'Oh, Frannie...' he whispered.

She looked at him gravely. 'I'm still a little scared, but let's try.'

He reached down again to touch her, but she pushed his fingers away impatiently, pulling him on top of her. He rubbed against her, feeling her throb beneath him, then he drew back and forced himself against her slick hardness, finding resistance all the way; she was so tight he could barely progress. Her face was pale, and she broke into a sweat. He knew he was hurting her, at some awful fundamental level, but he didn't stop. He drove himself into her. She was hot, and still wet from her orgasm. He reached down and picked up the towel he'd thrown to the floor earlier, lifting her bottom and pushing it beneath her. She looked up, agony in her eyes, and braced as he fell into her in an unbelievable dreamlike pleasure-pain as she tightened still further around him, her pain making her contract. He was so stimulated that he hardened again instantly, and realised that they were trapped together. He looked at her face. It was panicked.

'Relax, I've heard that this happens sometimes. Just relax.'

'It hurts,' she spat.

'Just this time, it won't hurt you ever again. Let me kiss you. We're not going anywhere, just hold me, and don't think about it.'

He watched as that old familiar sarcastic expression came over her face. 'Don't *think* about it? I've got what feels like Blackpool Tower inside me, and you're telling me not to *think* about it?'

He shut her up with a kiss, laughing. She laughed too, and he felt her relax. He thought about Blackpool, about seagull shit on the prom, about the odd floating material in the sea, about the stink of old people sheltering in bus stops, and he realised he was shrinking inside her. He carefully withdrew, desperate not to hurt her any more. He wiped himself with the towel that had caught her blood and his seed, and he folded it away carefully.

'Why are you doing that?' she asked.

'It's our business, nobody else's,' he replied.

Fight for the Future

She nestled close to him. 'I was going to put my new nightie on...'

'Don't,' he said sleepily. 'This is wonderful.' He pulled her towards him, relishing her nakedness next to him, and fell asleep. She closed her eyes, and joined him in their dreams.

Chapter 18

Frances stood on the beach, watching her husband set up a deckchair. He'd flatly refused to hire one for himself, assuring her that they were 'monstrosities'.

'Put that windbreak up next,' she said anxiously.

'Your wish is my command,' he said, suiting actions to words.

The young couple had found a reasonably large empty space on the hot sand of Blackpool beach. Frannie waited until the windbreak was up, then crouched down a little.

'Hold that towel up in front of me,' she hissed.

'Why?' Anthony asked.

'Because I'm taking my dress off.'

'Ah,' he said, and stood facing her, holding the towel out.

'Turn round!' she said.

'Why?'

'Because ... oh ... just turn round, please?'

He shrugged, and turned round, smiling pleasantly at passers-by.

The tide continued to go out. Eventually she spoke. 'All right, you can look now.'

He turned back and raised his eyebrows. 'Frannie, I saw you put that swimsuit on under your dress this morning. Why make me turn round?'

'It's different on the beach,' she told him, as if he was being deliberately dim.

He lay down on the sand, smiling wickedly.

'That's a nice cossie. You look great in red.'
She blushed. 'Get lost, Anthony.'
'Oh, I couldn't possibly, I think I know my way around far too well.' He let his gaze crawl across her body for a second or two, and then looked up, licking his lips wolfishly and meeting her increasingly embarrassed stare. He winked extravagantly.
'Stop leering,' she told him.
'How can it be leering when we've been married for three years? Let's go back to the room,' he suggested.
'Anthony, we can't. I've explained. We have to stay out all day. We can't go back until teatime.'
He frowned. 'OK, let's get another room somewhere else. Forget the B&B, let's book into a proper hotel. This is our holiday, and we've got money.'
'That's for emergencies,' she told him.
He looked at her gravely. 'Frances, I think this could *be* an emergency.'
She looked at him, unamused. 'Anthony, please try to be respectable.' She took a magazine out of her bag and started to read it.
He looked at her for a minute, hoping for some attention, and then sighed and took off his shirt. She peered over the top of her magazine for a moment, and then hid behind it as he glanced at her. He stood up, kicked off his shoes, peeled off his socks, and started to undo his jeans. As he let them slip down his legs, she hissed, 'Anthony, what *do* you think you're doing?'
He stood in front of her, modelling a

frighteningly bright pair of blue patterned shorts.

'Wearing the latest fashion in swimming trunks,' he told her.

'Good grief,' she said. She didn't elaborate, and returned to her magazine. He reached around her into the bag, taking out a bottle of sun oil, and liberally applied it to his legs and chest. 'Rub this into my back, will you?' he said.

She sighed and sat up, patiently rubbing the warm oil into his back. When she had finished, he turned round and said. 'Your turn.'

'I'll do it myself,' she told him primly.

'Spoilsport.' He glanced at her white legs. 'Do it soon, you'll burn otherwise.'

She grabbed the bottle from him, applying the oil and only asking for help with the back of her neck, lifting her hair while he rubbed it into her skin.

Satisfied, he lay down on his back, and started to soak up the sun. He listened happily as her breathing changed, and she dozed off. He made a mental note to wake her up before she got too much sun, and closed his eyes.

A shadow fell across him, and he opened his eyes, scowling. He looked up to see a dark-haired child watching him. He guessed she was about two or three years old.

'Hello, you. Where's your mum?' he asked.

She said nothing, just stared.

'What's your name?' he asked.

She didn't reply. He sat up and looked around. None of the families or young couples on the beach looked alarmed or concerned.

'Are you lost?' he asked her.

'Lost,' she said confidingly, and held out her hand.

He nudged his wife. 'Frances, there's a little girl here who's lost.'

She screwed up her eyes. 'There's a lost children cabin on the prom. Near the toilets. Take her there.'

'Will you come with us?'

'No. I'm sunbathing.' When she used that tone he knew it was pointless to argue.

He stood up, reaching for his shirt and putting it on, leaving it unbuttoned. He smiled at the little girl.

'Follow me then,' he said. She held out her hand, looking at him, and he took it. 'OK. Right. Prom. That's the road bit at the top, isn't it? Come with me, we'll get you back to Mummy and Daddy.'

He found the lost children cabin easily enough, and knocked on the door. A large woman with coarse blonde hair in a bun let them in. She knelt down to speak to the child. 'What's your name then?'

The girl shook her head, and gripped Anthony's hand tighter. The attendant looked up. 'Where did you find her?'

Anthony described the spot on the beach, and looked hopefully at the woman. 'Do I leave her here?'

'Yes, I'll give her a lollipop, and she can wait here.' She nodded briskly. 'Just leave your name and address. If nobody claims her in twenty-four hours, then you can keep her.'

Anthony stared at her for a couple of seconds, then laughed. 'Joke? Right?'

'Yes, joke. I'm Mrs Williams. Don't worry about her, we get dozens of lost souls every day.'

Anthony tried to disentangle his hand from the little girl's, but she was holding on tightly. He knelt down. 'Come on, honey, let go of my hand. I've got to get back to my wife. Mrs Williams will look after you.'

The girl looked at him, and her lip started to tremble. Anthony was trying to think of a way to persuade her to release him when the door flew open, and a red-haired man rushed in.

'Thank goodness, you're here.' He took the child by the other hand, and started to explain to the attendant that he was the child's uncle, they were up from London for a week, she didn't know the beach, and that he'd only taken his eye off her for just one minute. Mrs Williams looked at the child's face, and the way she was trying to hide behind the good-looking young man who had brought her in.

'Where on the beach did you leave her?' she asked.

'Just near the North Pier, my brother and his wife have gone to do some shopping. I was looking after her. Honestly, you take your eyes off them for a minute and they're off.'

'The child was found a good way from there. And she doesn't seem to know you. Have you got anything that says you're her uncle? I'm sorry to have to be like this, but it's my job.'

Fight for the Future

The 'uncle' glared at her. 'You old bat. Look, if I'm not there with her when her parents get back, they'll be sick with worry. Can't you tell we're related?'

Anthony spoke up. He kept his voice level. 'Why don't you go back, and wait for her parents? The little girl will be fine here with this lady until they turn up. And please don't speak to the lady like that, there's no need for it.'

'And who the bleeding hell are you?' challenged the other man.

The attendant saw a dangerous light in Anthony's eyes, but observed that he instinctively moved to make sure that he was between the child and the man who claimed to be her uncle.

She spoke calmly. 'Actually, that's a good idea. You go back to where you lost her, and wait for her parents, then you can bring them straight here. By the way, I won't put up with any nonsense in here. If the two of you are spoiling for a fight, you can take it outside, or I'll call for the police. Do you understand?'

'Yes, ma'am,' said Anthony. He glanced behind him. The little girl was gazing up at him.

'Right then. I'll be back, with her parents. Then we'll see who's sorry.' The man stormed out of the cabin.

Anthony took a seat next to the child. The attendant shook her head. 'Well, she's certainly taken to you. It looks like you're staying for a while. Would you like a lollipop too?'

Anthony tried to get the child to speak to

him, but she just wandered around the room, inspecting the books and toys, glancing backwards every few seconds to make sure he was still there, occasionally making her way back to sit next to him. Every time she sat down she took his hand. He was sure the blonde woman was laughing at him.

Other children came and went, some crying, some hysterical, some quite clearly returnees who wanted a free lollipop. They were all dealt with efficiently, and returned quickly to parents whose moods varied from panicked to exasperated.

Eventually, the door opened again and the uncle strode in, followed by a young couple around Anthony's age. The husband was quite tall, very thin, with straight limp sandy hair. Anthony's instincts kicked in, and he realised that he liked the guy. The wife was about Anthony's own height, with thick dark-brown hair and hazel eyes. She looked around and summed the situation up instantly. She watched her brother-in-law with barely hidden irritation as he tried to explain the situation.

'She's here. This...' He saw the expression on Anthony's face. 'This *lady* wants proof that you're her parents.'

Mrs Williams smiled. The child had wrapped her arms around her dad's legs.

'Daddy,' she said, happily. Anthony felt a hard, hot moment of jealousy, and bit it down. Her father lifted her up and hugged her while her mother signed a form and walked across the room. She favoured Anthony with a dazzlingly brilliant smile.

'Thank you for bringing her here. She's a real

Fight for the Future

handful sometimes. We won't leave her again, I promise you. I'm sure you've got better things to do with your holiday than look after stray children.'

'No, really, it was a pleasure. She's lovely.'

The woman brightened. 'Have you got any of your own?'

Anthony returned the smile, liking her straightforward confidence. 'No, not yet. Soon, I hope.'

'Well, I'm sure you'll be a great dad. Joyce is very shy with men, usually.'

She waved goodbye, following her husband and brother-in-law out of the cabin. Anthony heard her raise her voice as she left.

'Joyce Bridget Foster! If you EVER do that again …'

Anthony left the close, dark cabin, and made his way back to Frances.

Chapter 19

Tomas jumped off the train at Lancaster and made his way out of the station to the bus stop. In his pocket he held that precious letter from home. 'Everyone well, but take care. We love you' it said. He would show it to his twin, and they would send a letter back to a post office a few dozen miles from where their parents lived. Since they'd left home, their parents had moved, they didn't know to where.

He longed to see them again, to tell them about Miriam and Frances, to tease his sisters. He wondered what they looked like as wolves, and daydreamed about his parents, smiling wryly at a memory of his first run with his father. He patted the letter again.

A hand on his shoulder made him spin around, his arm lifting to defend himself. His assailant pushed him against the wall of the bus shelter, reaching into his pocket and removing the letter. Tomas tried to fight back, but the man was strong. The stranger looked to be in his forties and foreign. He was dark like Tomas.

The young man realised that this stranger looked a lot like himself: the same dark curls, the same heart-shaped face, the same long-lashed dark eyes. He swallowed.

'Who are you?'

'Miguel. And if I was Harald, you'd be dead. You have to do better, brother.'

Tomas relaxed. He had heard of his older brother, but had never met him, hadn't even been sure that he was still alive. His parents' eldest sons had left home long before he and Anthony had been born; they had been twenty-seven years older than him.

'Why are you here? Are Mama and Papa in danger?' he tried to disguise the awe he felt for this man who had been the stuff of legends throughout his childhood. Miguel had fought in the Second World War, finding positions that would take him within reach of the White Pack territory, and making raids on them. His twin had died within months of leaving home. The two of them had been following rumours of a werewolf woman in Italy, and had been ambushed by a group of White Pack men. The woman had never been found. Miguel had never settled, making revenge his life's work.

The older man shrugged. 'They're well enough. Mama is pining for you. I met her, by chance, in a market. I didn't know they were living so close to me. I moved away again, naturally. But she wanted me to find you, to make sure you were safe.'

Tomas was insulted. 'We're doing fine. We have wives, almost certainly half-bloods! We have jobs, homes, money.'

Miguel scowled. 'And you let yourself be followed from the post office in Manchester to the bus stop that takes you home to those homes and wives! Incredible! If I had been Harald, I would be an hour away from killing you all!'

Tomas shook his head. 'Who's this Harald?'

Miguel nodded. 'I shall tell you. We'll move away from the bus stop, eh? I won't go home with you, but we'll eat together.'

Tomas led his eldest brother to a chip shop down a side street. They found a table, Miguel automatically checking the exits and lines of sight before sitting with his back to the wall.

'Harald is the bright young star of the White Pack. He has sworn to finish what his father and grandfather began: the eradication of rogues. That is you and me, you understand?'

Tomas shuddered. 'We're safe here, surely?'

'No, you are not safe. I knew where this letter was to be delivered to. It was easy to wait until it was collected. You are so easily recognisable as our mother's son. What if Harald had done the same? What if he had followed you, secretly, to your home, your wife? You must be more careful.' The older man turned his head away as the waitress arrived and took their order.

Tomas shrugged. 'Then we'll be more careful. Will you come back with me? Anthony would love to meet you, you are his hero.'

'Tomas, have you been listening to me? We are in mortal danger. You really do not want me to know where you live, what your wife looks like, or anything about your twin. You can't trust anyone, you must understand. Anyone.'

Tomas sat back, disappointed. 'Can you tell me about anyone from home? We miss them so much.'

'Everyone is still alive and well, but scared. We're the last, we are sure of it. Every other family is long extinct, the work of the Whites again. None of us have found mates. Sylvia is going to marry a normal, she wants a family. Audrey will do the same, when she finds the right man. We're scattering as widely as we can now. The continuation of our kind will need a miracle.'

Tomas spoke. 'Is there anything we can do to help? We can fight, we practise still.'

'You do what?' Miguel's voice conveyed a dull horror. 'You change? Where? Why? Are you so stupid?'

'We can't forget who we are, Miguel. Don't worry, we have a safe place, a farm.'

'No, no, no. Don't tell me these things. Tomas, for the last time... I tell you, all our lives are in danger. Our only hope is to hide for as long as possible, to try to ride out this storm, to hope that the White Pack will weaken. Even I hide now. I fear they will learn things from me if they capture me.'

'Why did you come?' Tomas said, quashed.

'To warn you about Harald. He's cunning, and ruthless.' Miguel looked up as the meals arrived. He waited until the waitress had gone, and then smiled. 'And to let you know that you are missed by our parents and sisters. Mama sends her love, she said that Papa misses you. But you are not to come home, you are safest here, it was a good choice. The Whites' last concerted attack in this country was comprehensive and almost completely successful. They believe that they can ignore Britain. Stay here, stay secret, and you will survive.'

'And the rest of the family?'

'None of us want to die,' Miguel said, looking

his brother in the eye. 'I do wish I could stay and get to know you, brother, but it would bring danger to you.'

'I understand,' Tomas said briefly. They ate their meals quickly, in silence. Miguel was looking at him fondly.

'I hope you make it. I hope one day we can meet again, in safety. Brothers should meet more than once in a lifetime. Good luck, Tomas. Don't follow me.'

Tomas put down his knife and fork. 'Shall I write a reply for you to take home?' he said.

'No! Post it as usual. Do not forget to tell Anthony everything I've told you. You understand?'

Tomas's face took on an unaccustomed level of seriousness. 'I do, it took me a while, but I do understand. Thank you for coming, for the warning. We'll stay low, stay quiet.'

'Goodbye, brother. I'll leave you to pay for the meal.' Miguel winked, briefly playful, and Tomas recognised the expression. He didn't stand, or make a fuss. It would be best not to be remembered.

He went back to Bardale by the long route, changing buses three times until he was sure he wasn't being followed, and only then going home. Later that evening, he stood in the back garden, kicking a football lightly against the back wall of the house. It was the signal he and Anthony employed to say that they wanted to speak to each other without going through the social niceties of speaking to each other's wives. Within a few minutes the back door opened and Anthony stepped out. He closed the

Fight for the Future

door quietly and walked across to Tomas. There was a low fence between the two properties, with a permanently opened gate in it.

'Did you get it?' Anthony asked.

'I got it. Miguel tailed me,' Tomas said briefly, quietly.

'Miguel? Our brother Miguel?' Anthony grinned. 'Is he coming here?'

'No way. I got told off. We're not being careful enough. There's some bugger called Harald who is stirring trouble at home. And things are getting worse, not better. We've to lie low, no more mentioning the fact that we're married, definitely. Don't write anything that could be useful to an enemy. Basically, it's going to be "We're still alive, are you?" from now on.'

'Shit.'

'Yes, shit and more shit. The good news is that so far as Miguel knows, everyone is fine. Here, read the letter. It just says "alive and well", but you'll want to see it, I know.'

He passed the letter to his twin, who studied it longingly, wanting to hear his parents' voices again. He crumpled it into a ball and thrust it into his pocket. 'I'll burn it,' he said.

'Yeah.' They stood for a while, hands in pockets, looking at the sky.

'We're not to change either. He was clear about that.'

'*What?* Are we to stop breathing too?' Anthony was appalled.

'If we have to, we have to, he understands,

but not for fun. Just when it gets too much, you know? It's probably best to do it only one at a time, the other standing guard and making sure that we're not observed.'

'This is serious. Maybe we should be making plans?'

'I think so. Let's think about it, and talk again tomorrow?'

'Yes, OK.' Anthony hugged his brother briefly, and then shivered. The night was cool. He went back inside, thinking hard.

Chapter 20

Anthony stood back to admire his work. The new henhouse was clean, well built, and fox-proof. Unlike the old one, it was high enough for a man to walk in without stooping.

'That's a good job, lad,' his father-in-law said. 'We'll mek a farmer of thee yet.'

Anthony shook his head. 'I don't think it's my vocation, and Frannie has no ambitions to be a farmer's wife.'

'Aye, I'll pass the farm on to Maisie, I think. She's cut out for it, nothing fazes her.'

'Good plan.' Anthony said absently, uninterested.

Eddie shrugged; the young man clearly had other things on his mind. 'How is Frances?' he asked.

'Huge, tired out. I keep making her walk around the garden, just to get a bit of exercise. She's still working though. It's a good job it's just playing with numbers. It keeps her happy.' Anthony smiled, knowing that Eddie would recognise the teasing.

'Bloody big numbers, some of them,' Eddie commented. Frannie had taken some courses, and now worked at home doing the books for several local businesses. She had a good reputation for speed and accuracy, and was much sought after. A year earlier, she had found herself in the enviable position of having to turn away potential customers. Anthony had stepped in and suggested that she raise her fee at that point. To her pleasure, and his, she was now earning as much as he was.

'Cuppa?' Anthony suggested. Eddie agreed, and they went into the farmhouse. As they sat down the phone started to ring, and they both stood up. Before they could get there, Maisie answered it. She spoke for a while, and then put the phone down and came into the kitchen, smiling.

'I wish you'd keep your friends off the phone. Our Frannie might want to call!' complained Eddie.

'That *was* Frannie. She says can Anthony come home, please? And can they borrow the car, because she wants to go to the hospital. For some reason.' She beamed at her father and brother-in-law. 'Go on, both of you. I'll look after things here. Give her my love.'

Anthony hadn't heard anything past 'come home, please' and was halfway down the lane by the time Eddie had caught up with him in the car. 'Jump in, daft beggar!' Eddie called out, slowing down just enough for Anthony to open the door and hop into the passenger seat.

Eddie looked across. Anthony was white-faced, shaking. 'I should have listened to her. This whole idea is stupid. She's too fragile for this.'

'She'll be just fine, so long as you look after her,' said Eddie in a soothing tone.

'I will, I will. Faster, go faster Eddie.' Anthony peered through the windscreen at the road, almost willing the vehicle forward by sheer concentration. Just before Anthony reached complete hysteria, Eddie drew up in front of the two neat semi-detached houses. Anthony spilled out of the passenger door and stumbled up the path. Miriam had evidently seen him coming, and opened the door, cradling her own baby, five-month-old John.

'She's OK, take some time to breathe,' she said calmly.

Anthony stopped, breathing deeply. 'Are you all right?' he asked her.

'I'm fine, fit to be left alone anyway. I've asked someone to go round to tell Tomas that Frances is in labour. He'll come home early to help me with John.' She smiled. 'After all these years, we both have babies within months of each other. I hope they'll be good friends.' She stood in the doorway, smiling.

'Excuse me, could I get past?' he said politely. She laughed and moved away, allowing him and Eddie into the house. In the kitchen, Frances was leaning on the table with both hands. She was quiet and pale, and her hair hung over her face. She looked up at Anthony, smiling, and the world faded away – all he could see was her. He stood transfixed, until she spoke. 'It's coming quickly, please get me to the hospital.'

Before she could breathe again she was in his arms and out of the house, the car door was open and she found herself sitting in the passenger seat next to her father. Anthony climbed into the back seat and reached forward to hold her hand. Eddie moved away carefully and they were on their way.

There was an unnatural silence; nobody spoke. At the hospital, Anthony gave all the details and Frances, perfectly silent, was examined and taken straight to the delivery room. A nurse tried to block

Anthony as he followed, but was politely ignored. The midwife saw the way that Frances was looking at her husband and signalled that he could stay. 'Do you want him here, love?' she asked.

Frances nodded as she undressed and changed into a hospital gown. Anthony accepted a gown and mask and sat next to her. He didn't take his eyes off her for a moment. The midwife looked at him. 'Is she mute?' she asked.

Anthony shook his head, and the midwife rolled her eyes. 'You are allowed to speak!' she said. Anthony let Frances take his hand and winced for a moment. He looked at the midwife. 'Years ago, we promised each other that we'd stop swearing in front of each other. I guess she's lost for words.' He looked back at Frances and was relieved to see her nod, as she clamped her lips shut.

The baby arrived quickly and messily, and the doctor called for a blood transfusion for Frances. Again, Anthony was officially sent away, but unofficially stayed because nobody could detach Frances's hand from his. He heard distractedly that the baby was tiny but healthy, and waited until the child was brought back, washed and wrapped, to be inspected.

'She's beautiful,' he said. 'Just like her mum.'

'He. It's a boy. But he is very pretty.' The nurse laughed at Anthony's embarrassment, but willingly handed the baby over.

'I'll be the best dad ever,' he vowed. The baby boy opened his mouth and screamed loudly. Anthony beamed exultantly, and held him until

Fight for the Future

Frances opened her eyes.

'Give him to me,' she whispered.

'I'll look after him, and you. Don't tire yourself out.' Anthony spoke clearly and authoritatively. Frances looked at him and held her arms out. 'If you want to look after us, you won't mither me. Give me my son. Now.'

Anthony watched as she inspected the baby carefully, intently. 'He's nothing like you,' she said, disappointed.

'No, he has your looks. What more could I wish for?'

She glanced up, blushing, still capable of being disarmed by him. 'What ... what do you think of Mark ... for a name?' she said hesitantly.

'Good, whatever you want. You could call him Hilda and I'd still love him,' he said soberly.

He watched as a tiny smile bloomed briefly on her face, then she looked at him again. 'Right you, go home and get the housework done. Mark and I are going to work out how I feed him, and then we're going to get some sleep.'

'But...'

'No buts, you're not staying. I need a rest, and you're distracting me. Go.'

He attempted his most charming smile, and opened his eyes wide. He really wanted to stay. She looked down, half laughing, and refused to look up again. Beaten, he turned and left.

Eddie sat outside. 'Well?'

Anthony looked at the older man. He was pale and held a twisted, bedraggled copy of the *Daily*

Mirror in his hands. He sat down next to him. 'They're both fine. I'm sorry, I thought someone would have told you.'

'I know it's a little lad,' Eddie said, then paused. Anthony felt there was something important that wasn't being said.

'What's the matter?' he asked.

Eddie looked round. 'It'll wait. Can I see her?'

'Not yet, she sent me away, she's exhausted. No, don't worry, she's fine, she was telling me off and bossing me about.'

Eddie laughed freely, relieved. 'Then I'll come back later. Shall we go back to your house? I could do wi' a cuppa.'

Back at the house, sitting at the kitchen table, Eddie finally spoke.

'T'kiddie. Is he like you?'

Anthony understood. 'I don't know. It's not like that. There's no way to really recognise each other – other than the change itself. I mean, if he's really sickly, he's probably half-blood, but I won't know for sure until he ... you know?'

'Turns into a wild animal,' Eddie muttered. 'And how soon does that happen?'

Anthony blinked. 'It's not like that, you know that. Aren't I well behaved on your land? Isn't Tomas?' It still felt odd to speak about this to a normal, but Eddie had kept their secret well, and rarely mentioned it. Anthony became more conciliatory.

'It usually happens for the first time when a

Fight for the Future

kid is about fourteen, it's part of growing up for our kind. Tomas and I were ready for it, we grew up with it as part of our lives. I'll have to keep a close eye on Mark and make sure I'm there for him when it happens.'

'So, tha's not going to tell him owt before then?'

'No, because he might not be like me. Why set him up for something that won't happen?' Anthony was wary about where the conversation was going.

Eddie bit the bullet. 'And if he isn't? If he grows up and never gets furry? Will you be disappointed?'

Anthony thought deeply; the man deserved an honest answer. 'Yes, I will be, for his sake. It's glorious, liberating, exciting. It teaches you things about yourself. I want my son to know what it's like. Not only that, if he's not like me, then he's going to be like Frances.' The implications were left unstated. 'But I'll still love him, whatever he is.'

Eddie nodded, and spoke again, cautiously aware of the capabilities of the man he was speaking to. 'I'm sorry lad, I've got to know. Will you try again, if t'kiddie turns out wrong?'

Anthony froze, stilling as he realised what Frances's father was implying. He spoke stiffly. 'I've told Frannie that I'm happy for Mark to be an only child. She's always said that she only wants one. I respect that. He'll grow up with his cousin, after all. You know that, we've all talked about it. So what are you saying? Are you asking if I'll try to force Frannie into having a late baby if Mark turns out not to be like me? Or are you asking if I'll try again with another woman?'

'I've got an idea of what you're like. It's not in your nature to settle for one kiddie, or even one lass.'

'Eddie, I've always respected you. And I know that you're asking these questions out of concern for Frannie. But you had better leave, now, before I lose my temper. The answer to all your questions is that I love Frances, make of that what you will. Goodbye, Eddie.'

'Aye, I'm sorry, but I had to ask. I'll sithee later.' Eddie stood and made his way to the door, aware of the growing fury of the man he had come to respect. As he left the house, he spoke to Tomas, who had just got home from work and was at the door.

'I've mebbe wound tha brother up a bit,' he said.

Tomas looked warily down the hall. Already he could hear the crashing of crockery and a low, furious growling. 'I'll see to him,' he said briefly, and waited until the farmer was in his car and halfway down the road before entering the house and locking the door behind him.

The black wolf stood on the kitchen table, in the middle of a mess of scattered crockery and ripped clothing. He was biting his own tail in frenzied frustration. Tomas righted an overturned chair and sat at the table, leaning back a little, looking his twin in the eye and waiting. Eventually, Anthony calmed down enough to change back and stand in the middle of the kitchen, still furious.

'Hello,' said Tomas. 'Who rattled your cage?'

'Fucking bastard suspicious bastard FUCKER!' Anthony screamed, then breathed deeply. 'What more do I have to do? I've got a job, I get up early, I go to bed early, I've not killed anything for MONTHS! I BLOODY WELL MARRIED HER! What more do they want from me? I bloody well love her. I love the baby.' He shut up for a moment, and picked up his jeans, looking ruefully at the burst waistband and the ripped legs. 'I hate doing that,' he said sadly.

Tomas smiled, meeting Anthony's eyes and gently touching the tips of his own ears. 'Furry bits,' he said helpfully. Anthony touched his own ears, finding them still pointed and furry and overly large. 'Bloody hell. I can't even do that properly now! Hang on.' He concentrated hard, and soon had his human ears back. He smiled weakly at his twin. 'You have a nephew, by the way. Mark. He's beautiful. Utterly, wildly, darkly beautiful.' He breathed deeply. 'And that IDIOT Eddie implied that I wasn't happy with him, or with my Frances.'

Tomas shrugged. 'He's Frannie's dad, and the baby's grandad. He's going to be feeling protective.'

'That's my job, not his,' snapped Anthony. 'I am not going to leave them.'

Tomas looked at his hands, and spoke quietly. 'Are you sure? I mean, I love Miriam more than anything in the world, and John is my life, but if a wolf woman turned up here, now ... I'm not sure how I'd react.'

'I'm sure,' replied his twin, soberly. 'Frances trusts me. She learned to trust me, and it wasn't easy. I won't ever let her down.' The ghost of a smile flitted across his face. 'She's not Miriam.'

Tomas shrugged, he understood. 'John's mine, nobody can deny that. And Miriam loves me, in her own way.'

Anthony looked at his twin cautiously, and then put the kettle on and went upstairs. He returned within minutes, dressed in fresh clothes. Tomas was still sitting at the table, drumming his fingers.

'We don't talk often enough, about the important things,' Anthony ventured.

Tomas looked up, his eyes becoming distant, veiled. 'I said, I love her. That's enough.'

'She's cheating on you again, isn't she?'

Tomas looked at the ceiling. 'She says it's not cheating if I know about it. I really would prefer not to know about it, you know? Although it's not as if I'm a perfect angel, is it?'

Anthony shrugged. Whether Tomas or Miriam had first been unfaithful had become immaterial. They seemed to be in some sort of bizarre infidelity competition, and rumours were already beginning to fly around the village. A large dent in the plastered wall of the White Bull matched perfectly with the shape of the head of a young man who had dared to inform Tomas that Miriam was too good to be married to a 'dago plumber'. Tomas had got away with that one; the local constable had been drinking in the bar at the time and had seen the whole thing, and approved of Tomas's actions.

'Are you really unhappy?' Anthony asked cautiously.

'Unhappy? No! I adore her, she loves me. I guess we're just too much alike. Maybe it's not a conventional marriage, but we can deal with it. And, as I said, nobody can doubt that John is mine. I've got what I wanted.' He looked up, suddenly struck by a thought. 'Unless he's yours, of course. Miriam always did want that particular itch scratched.'

'No, she only tested those waters once, before you were married. She's yours, I'm Frannie's and don't take it the wrong way, but I'm not even tempted.' He finished his cup of tea and started to tidy up the mess he had made. 'I'm not sure I can keep this up for the rest of my life – this hiding, not changing, not running, not hunting. It's driving me crazy.'

'It's keeping us alive,' Tomas pointed out. 'And keeping our wives and children alive too.'

'Damn, I know. I suppose that's why I lost it just then. I could almost hear freedom galloping away from me. Weird really, when this is exactly what we planned for and hoped for.'

'Will it be enough though?' asked Tomas. 'Even if both our lads are like us, will it be enough?'

'That's up to them. We can't do any more than we have.' Anthony carried the ruined clothes and crockery out to the dustbin. 'I suppose we could watch the bloodlines, keep an eye out for known carriers having more kids, but all that is for the future.' He turned to his twin. 'Thanks for coming round. I'm going to get back to the farm now, to sort things out with Eddie. I still think he should have kept his nose out of my business, but I suppose he had good reasons.'

Tomas stood, asking him if it would be all right if he and Miriam went to the hospital later to see their new nephew. Anthony grinned, and started talking again about how beautiful his son was. 'I really honestly don't care at the moment if he's furry or half-blood, he's wonderful...' The amused look on his twin's face stopped him. 'OK, I know, you were exactly the same when John was born, and I told you to shut up more than once. But he is amazing.'

Tomas stayed silent, smiling, and turned and left.

Chapter 21

Frances heard the front door slam shut, and stood up, alarmed. She wasn't expecting anyone. She glanced quickly at the two boys playing with Lego under the kitchen table, and hurried out into the hall. Tomas stood there, his thick overcoat wet through with rain.

'Tomas, what's happened? Take your coat off, you look terrible. Are you OK? Has there been an accident?'

Her brother-in-law took his coat off and silently followed her into the kitchen, sitting down in the chair that she'd just vacated. The boys peeked out and smiled at him, before going back to their game.

'Where's Anthony?' Tomas asked.

'At the farm, him and Dad are getting some stock ready for market. Why? What's happened? Are you all right?'

'I need to talk to Anthony,' Tomas said shakily. He peered under the table, forcing himself to put on a face for the boys. 'Where's Miriam? Has she left you babysitting?'

'She's gone shopping. It's no problem, really, the boys are easier to look after when they're together.' She lit the flame under the kettle. 'Aren't you going to tell me?'

Tomas took a deep breath. 'I'll tell Anthony.' He winced, expecting her to complain, but she merely shrugged.

'He'll tell me then. It's as broad as long. Tea or coffee?'

'Oh, tea please.' He peered under the table again, sticking his tongue out at his son. John giggled with delight and started to crawl out. Mark followed cautiously, and within seconds both boys were sitting on Tomas's lap. He glanced at the table, at the ledgers and receipts that sat neatly in trays.

'You're working. Do you want me to take the boys home? I can come back with them later,' he offered.

'No, stay. Anthony will be back within the hour, I'm sure.' The kettle boiled and she warmed the teapot with half a cup of water, before spooning in the tea and filling it with hot water. She stuck a crocheted tea cosy over the top, and left the tea to brew for a while.

She took a seat on the other side of the table from her brother-in-law, and drew her work back towards her. 'You don't mind if I carry on? This has to be finished tomorrow,' she said.

'No, no. Carry on. I'm sorry I interrupted you. Miriam's got a bit of a cheek leaving John here when you're working. Do you want me to say something to her?'

She looked up, a pained expression taking shape. 'Tomas, I've said before that Mark is easier to look after when John's here. Miriam does her fair share of looking after the pair of them. Now, will you pour that tea while I finish this job?'

Tomas flushed and apologised. Without any choice in the matter, he sat quietly playing with the boys while Frances worked. She glanced at the clock occasionally, taking sips of tea. He watched her quietly. They were rarely alone together and he was still curious about the woman his twin had married. She had seemed so much younger than them, until the day she returned from the honeymoon and efficiently took over her own house. He often felt a little intimidated by her; he could rarely make her laugh, and she seemed immune to his attempts to charm her. However, his brother valued her, that much was clear, and for Anthony's sake he had always managed to maintain a friendly relationship with her.

He noticed, as he helped the boys to build a house with the Lego bricks, that both of them looked up frequently to check where she was, and he thought about how John and Mark were effectively getting the benefits of a pack upbringing. For a moment, he was acutely jealous. His own parents had, by necessity, been a single-pair pack. His childhood had been punctuated by fights between his increasingly frustrated parents, who had both grown up in true packs, and never stopped wanting more mates. By living so close together, he and Anthony had provided a family for their sons that included two fathers and two mothers. The boys seemed to be thriving on it, naturally treating all four adults as parents. Perhaps it was an indication that they were full-blood werewolf children, or perhaps he was just reading too much into a family situation that must be repeated in normal human families.

Both boys were walking and talking now. Mark was a graceful, intense, dark-haired child, who was beginning to break free of a tendency to follow

John's every suggestion, and to come up with ideas of his own. John was a cheerful, sunny, uncomplicated little lad, who accepted the good things in life eagerly, and the bad things stoically. Neither of them had thrown a tantrum in their lives, to his knowledge. As Tomas watched them, he wondered what effect his news would have on them. He had no idea how to deal with what had happened.

As he brooded, fighting down the memories that he knew would lead to terror, he heard the front door open. A cheerful shout of, 'I'm home, get the kettle on!' made him smile reluctantly. The kitchen door was flung open and Anthony stopped in surprise, seeing Tomas in the chair that he was expecting Frances to be in. Tomas noticed with a pang that his twin looked for Frances before stopping to hug him. It was clear who was now most important in Anthony's life. Frannie was already clearing her books away and making for the kettle, and the children were dragging Anthony to the building bricks to show him what they'd created. Anthony was happy, and Tomas really did not want to tell him the news. He was wondering how and when he was going to broach the subject when Frances did it for him.

'Tomas has something important to tell you. I'll take the kids into the other room while you talk. The kettle's on.'

'Oh, thanks love.' Anthony got up from the floor and sat down opposite his twin, looking at him expectantly. When it became obvious that Tomas was waiting for Frances and the children to be out of earshot, he frowned. He started to speak and was shushed by Tomas. Eventually Tomas began.

'I guess they can't hear us. We could go to my house, I suppose, but I know I can trust Frannie not to listen in.'

'Listen in to what?'

'Miguel is dead,' Tomas said. He wondered, as he said it, how he was managing to keep his voice so clear and calm.

'Miguel? How? How do you know? Are you sure? Was it in the letter?'

'I saw it,' he whispered. He met Anthony's eyes. 'I saw him killed. I don't know what to do.'

Anthony's face was grim. 'Tell me everything. From the start,' he said.

Tomas nodded, organising the events of the day in his mind. 'I was careful, Anthony, I swear I was careful. I changed trains, and arrived in Manchester on the Blackburn train.'

Anthony nodded. They'd stopped arriving in Manchester on the Preston train since Miguel's warning.

'I walked around for a while, checking things out. I didn't see anything to be suspicious about so I approached the post office carefully. They must have been hiding ... of course they were hiding. I was just about to move into the open when I saw Miguel. He walked straight out of the shadows, showing his face, throwing his shoulders back. He was wet through with the rain straight away, but anyone who'd heard the slightest rumour of his name would have identified him.' Tomas smiled thinly. 'Anthony, he was a walking legend. I've never seen such a man. He had such presence. Everyone turned to look at him as he walked across that street.'

Anthony closed his eyes, imagining the scene. Tomas continued. 'I almost called to him, before I realised what he was doing. He was making sure that he was seen. I realised that meant he knew there was someone there to see him. I hung back, I watched. God help me, Anthony, I stood there and watched.'

'Did he know you were there?' Anthony asked grimly.

'Yes, I believe he did. He didn't look at me, but he stepped out of the shadows just as I was going to. He must have been waiting for me.'

'What happened then?'

'Ah. It was a dance. It was a busy street, you understand? Six men, six brothers, they converged on him. There was no fuss, no cry. They walked past, they each struck a blow. They were gone in seconds. Our brother fell, he knew it was the end. I wanted to go to him. I've never wanted anything more in my life, Anthony, you must understand that!'

'I do. Are you sure he died?'

'He was dead. I'm sure. Each blow drew his lifeblood. Each blow looked, at first, like a fist striking his body, but each fist concealed a blade. He bled to death so very quickly. The six who killed him scattered and were gone.' Tomas paused.

'Anthony, he died for us. He must have known, somehow, that there would be an ambush for me or for you. He made an irresistible target of himself, he waited until he knew that I would see and understand. It's over. The White Pack know that we're here. He died to show us that, and to protect us. If he would do that, we must be the last ones alive.'

Anthony reached across the table and took his twin's hand. 'Are you sure you weren't followed?' he asked cautiously. 'I have to ask, you know that?'

'I went five stops in the wrong direction, I caught a bus west, I walked five miles to a train station. I went to Liverpool. Then I came home. I waited each time. In Liverpool I stood in the open and waited to die. I wasn't followed. I doubt they even saw me in Manchester. It was as if Miguel cast a spell, they could see nothing but him.'

'Did he fight back?' Anthony said dully.

'No. It was a sacrifice, for us, for our family.'

'But why would he just stand there and wait to die? He is ... he was ... a soldier.' Anthony frowned.

Tomas shrugged. 'Maybe he didn't want to be seen fighting. A great warrior fighting six men would draw more attention than an unsolved murder. And if he had fought, could he have resisted the instinct to change, to become a wolf and fight for his life? He died to hide us, to warn us.' Tomas looked up, despairing. 'What do we do now?'

Anthony was pale, the life had gone out of him. He shook his head and stood, looking out of the kitchen window at the scrap of garden, the neat privet hedge, the lawn that was tidy, but scuffed around the see-saw that he'd bought the Christmas before for Mark and John. He stared at the flowering cherry sapling that was just beginning to thrive and thicken. Tomas realised uneasily that his twin was committing the scene to his memory. Anthony turned.

'We have to hide our family, and disappear. We have to do everything possible to put distance between us and them. We endanger them. Our faces are known. We are the last survivors. If the Whites knew there was a letter waiting for us, that must mean our parents are dead.' He spoke flatly. Tomas winced, but accepted the truth of it. Anthony continued. 'We don't have much time. They know we are within travelling distance of Manchester. They know we are twins, foreign to this area. They know, to a reasonable degree, what we look like. They don't know the surname we're using, because our parents write using our real name – that's one good thing, but I wish we'd changed our first names too. There are many of them, they have resources. They may even know about Bardale, and guess that we would come here. We have to assume they will find us if we stay here. They will kill us. They will kill Frances and Miriam, they will kill Mark and John. You understand?'

Tomas opened his mouth to protest, but remembered the almost gleeful callousness with which Miguel's murderers had acted, and he accepted Anthony's judgement. 'What do we do?' he said quietly.

'Keep our secret from the women. Nobody will benefit from that particular truth. We need their trust, and we will not gain it by confessing to the lie we've told since the beginning. Do you agree?'

Anthony's brown eyes darkened almost to black. Tomas assented.

Anthony continued. 'We'll tell them that we are in mortal danger from the enemies from home that we came here to avoid. That much is true. We will let them draw their own conclusions. I will have to explain this to Eddie. We will need his help and his understanding. He will be angry and disappointed, but he knows what we are. I trust him. I need to know if you do too.'

'I do,' Tomas said, watching Anthony's face harden, his posture become more erect. For the first time, he saw the warrior within his gentle twin. He shuddered.

'We have to make sure the women are safe, and that they understand the extent of the danger. Then we leave, and we cannot come back until the White Pack is no longer a threat.'

'That may never happen,' hissed Tomas.

Anthony smiled wryly. 'I know that.' He filled a glass with water and took a long drink from it. 'When we are far enough from those we love, we start to kill. We take the life of every White Pack soldier, spy, or lost wanderer that we see. We make it our mission in life to avenge our family. We will protect our children by being as far from them as we can get, and by killing as many of our enemies as we can. I want blood, Tomas. I don't expect to survive for long, but I have a reckoning to make. Are you with me?'

'Always,' said his twin clearly, standing and embracing him.

'Go home, take John, explain things to Miriam. I'll speak to Frances.'

Anthony sat alone for a while after his twin left, sick to the stomach. Eventually, he stood and put the kettle on, going through the ritual of making tea. Drawn to the sound of the whistling kettle, Frances came into the kitchen. She looked at his face, and sat down hard. He looked at her, at the sharp planes of her face, the sleek length of her dark hair, the depths of her eyes. He was dizzied, and watched her lips move for a while without comprehension. Eventually, her irritation showed, and she spoke more loudly.

'Anthony. What is happening? What happened to Tomas?'

He met her gaze. 'I have to leave.'

She knew immediately what he meant. He watched silently as she waited a moment, helplessly, for him to take it back. Then came the anger, deepening to a dark fury, a loathing of herself and him that broke his heart there and then. For a moment, he saw a path for both of them. He could allow her this anger, this hatred, and he could be angry with her for doubting him. They could part this way, scabbing the hurt with self-righteous justifications. She could spend the rest of her life telling herself that she was better off without him, that he was a liar, a seducer, the fickle bastard that she had first suspected him to be. For a heartbeat, he saw that path ... and rejected it. She deserved better.

As she started to stand, to draw away from him, he reached across the table and took her hand, squeezing it gently. 'Frances, you didn't make any mistakes, my love.'

'Don't call me that,' she spat, hurting, already forcing the pain into a tight space inside her.

'But you *are* my love, my first love, my only love. And you were right to trust me, right to love me. I didn't trick you into loving me, don't think that.'

'So why are you leaving me?' She watched carefully as he stood. He didn't relinquish his hold on her hand. He moved around the table until they were face-to-face.

'Is Mark in bed?' he asked.

She blinked. 'Don't change the subject.'

He put his finger to her lips. 'Is he?'

'Not yet.'

'Let's put him to bed, then I'll tell you, and we can have the rest of the night to ourselves, without upsetting him. Can you do that?'

She straightened. 'Of course. Just promise me that there isn't another woman.'

'I promised till death do us part, remember?'

'I remember.'

Together they bathed Mark, who watched them curiously, aware of a change in things, but remained quiet. He was soon asleep. Anthony went back downstairs and locked the doors and windows. He tried to lighten his step as he went back upstairs to their bedroom, too aware of the heavy sound of his feet on each step.

Frances was sitting in front of the window, in the small chair that usually functioned as a coat stand.

She was looking at him, waiting for the explanation she was owed. He read her easily, as he always had; she was the picture of humiliated pride and self-loathing.

She spoke dully. 'Are you really going?'

'Yes. I don't want to, I swear.'

'Why?'

He swallowed. If he lied, she would know. He couldn't afford that. 'I can't tell you everything, but I'll tell you as much as I can. If you believe me, we stand a chance. If you don't, one or all of us will die.'

'Oh, for crying out loud!' she protested.

He waited, and she said no more.

'Tomas and I came here years ago, we didn't say where exactly we were from. We've never talked about the past, have we?'

'You didn't want to, that was clear,' she said wistfully.

'We came here to escape, to hide. That's perhaps something we should have told you, but it seemed crazy to worry you if we didn't have to.'

'Hide? From who? Are you in trouble? Did you desert from an army? Are you criminals?'

'No! We have enemies, hereditary enemies, really. It's a mad feud that we didn't start, and we don't want, but there are people out there who believe that Tomas and I have no right to be alive.'

'Is this true?'

'As true as my love for you,' he said, with a tiny smile. He watched her, and realised with a pang of gratitude that she accepted that statement without

Fight for the Future

question. He sat on the bed opposite her, taking her hands in his, leaning forward.

'We truly thought that if we fled, gave up any claim to life at home, hid far away in another country, they might leave us alone. But they won't. Tomas found out today that all our family back home are probably dead. He saw our brother die in front of him. Our enemies are crazy people.'

'This is the twentieth century, Anthony, this kind of thing doesn't happen.'

'Ah, for us it is, but these people don't think like us. The death of my family is a religious thing for them.'

'You do realise that this sounds like some ridiculous fairy story?' There was an edge of scorn in her words.

'It comes down to trust, of course. Do you trust me?'

'I don't know, not yet. You've just told me you're leaving me, and now you're telling me a tale straight from a storybook!'

'I have no proof, Frances. All I can say is that we have enemies, they have killed my parents, and at least one of my brothers. If they find us, they will kill us all – Tomas, Miriam, you, me, the boys.'

'No,' she said, standing and moving to the door, towards the small bedroom that held the sleeping toddler.

'Shhh, stay. Tonight, we'll bring him in with us, but for now, let him sleep.'

'Tonight? You think we might be in danger tonight?'

'Yes, we might. As long as you are with me, you are in danger. As long as you stay here, where you are known as my wife, you are in danger. I have to leave, and you have to move away.'

She looked at him speculatively. 'You can protect us,' she said, confidently.

'If I'm at work, I can't. I can't protect you against three, or six, or ten. I can't protect you if you and Mark are apart. I've thought it through and we have to split up, to protect you, and to protect our son.'

The sound of a fragile object smashing and breaking on the other side of the bedroom wall stopped him in his tracks, and they automatically shared a small smile. In that moment, he knew that she had believed him, and was making plans. She spoke. 'I guess Tomas is telling Miriam the same thing,' she said wryly. 'Will you stay with him?'

'We're going to draw attention away from you. They'll be looking for twins. If we stay together, they'll find us,' he said grimly. 'Your job is to disappear; can you do that?'

She looked at him for a long time, trying to think of a way around it. His face told the whole story. She gave up. 'Yes. I can. I'll go to Furness, there's lots of small businesses up there. I'll find work. Will you sign the house over to me? I'll need to sell it.'

'I'll sort it out first thing in the morning, together with the savings accounts and my bank account. It's all yours.' He smiled a little. 'You've not hit me yet,' he said.

She spoke deliberately, hardly believing her own words. 'I've decided that I believe you. Nobody would make something like this up. Just tell me again that our marriage has been real.'

'Frances, it has been, is, and always will be real.'

'That's good enough for me. When are you going?'

'I need to sign some kind of paper, I assume, to give you sole access to our account, and to give you permission to sell the house. Tomas will do the same with Miriam. I'll speak to your father, he deserves to know what's going on. Then we'll go. If possible, we'll do it tomorrow.'

'Tomorrow? You leave tomorrow?' Her voice faded, the hurt replaced by a lost, bewildered expression that unmanned him.

He swallowed, looking away, unable to bear it. 'We all leave tomorrow. You and Mark check into a hotel or a boarding house, not near here, not near Barrow. Stay there until you've found somewhere to buy. You can buy a new house when this place is sold.'

'What about Miriam? We can't split the boys up, they're like brothers.'

Anthony breathed deeply. 'I am so glad you think that. We'll all talk tomorrow, but I agree with you – you and Miriam should try to live within walking distance of each other. It's true, the boys will need each other, and you can help each other. You can talk to each other. You do realise that you will have to keep quiet about this forever? You'll have to assume that the danger won't go away.'

'Does that mean you're not coming back?' she whispered.

'I'll come back as soon as it's safe,' he said.

'And if it's never safe?' she challenged.

He pushed his fingers through his hair. 'Frannie, I don't have all the answers. I'm just going on instinct here, it's all new to me too. This wasn't planned. I'm just trying to figure out how to get you and Mark out of the shi— ... out of the mess that I've dropped you into.'

'We'll cope. What do I tell him?'

He had an answer for that. 'Don't tell him anything about this. Let him believe that I left you.'

'He'll hate you.'

'As long as he's not dead, I can deal with that. If he hates me, he won't try to find me when he's older.' He smiled thinly. 'I'll get as many cuddles as I can tomorrow. I might never get another. Hey, don't cry.'

'I don't believe this is happening,' his wife whispered. He watched, helpless, as Frances stood and walked out. He heard her in the bathroom, blowing her nose. He waited; he knew her.

Eventually she returned, her face scrubbed and clean. 'Just look into my eyes, and tell me that all this is the truth, that you love me, and that you'll come back if you can. Make me believe that, and I can cope with all of it.'

'It's the truth. I love you, and of course I want to come back. If I can be with you without putting you in danger, nothing will keep me away.'

Fight for the Future

She nodded, moving closer to him, closing her eyes. 'I could come with you. I could leave Mark with Maisie and Dad?'

He trembled for a moment, tempted. 'You'd do that? You could do that and be happy?'

'No, I wouldn't be happy. But I would do it, for you.' She snuggled deep into his arms, poised, waiting for his answer.

It came with a nervous laugh. 'No, Frances, I'm doing this for you. Don't steal my thunder. I want you to stay here with Mark. I want him brought up properly, by someone with brains and guts. Maisie's a good woman, but why would I want her to bring up my son when he could be with his beautiful brave mother?'

'Flatterer! You're teasing me. I might never spend another night with you, and you're teasing me again!'

'You love it.' He laughed.

'I love you,' she said, looking up, her eyes sparkling with laughter ... or tears – he could not tell.

It was a sombre band who made their way to the farm the following morning. Anthony took Eddie aside and told him everything, marvelling at the way the farmer accepted it.

'I'll understand if you find this difficult,' he said.

'Nay, I've always known there were trouble wi' your lot. That's why your great-gran ran off, eh? I hoped tha were well clear of it, but it's come again. You'll leave Frannie and t'kiddie wi' me?'

'No, I can't. Tomas and I made ourselves too well known around here. Folk will remember us for a long time, and if our enemies come here, they'll be on to Frannie and Mark with no mercy. She's going to hide, lie low. If I can come back, I will.' He shifted, uneasily.

'But tha won't, will thee? There'll be no coming back.'

'I don't think so,' Anthony confessed.

'Can I talk to her, keep in touch? On the phone?' demanded her father.

'Don't write the number down,' muttered Anthony, ashamed. 'You might be followed if you ever try visit them. They won't touch you, or the girls. They have a code, they won't hurt anyone without wolf blood.'

Eddie took a deep breath. 'Lose my lass to save her life? Is that what tha's tellin' me? I can't see her again?'

Anthony bit his lip. 'Please, it's the best way to protect her. The only way.'

Eddie stood up and walked to the mantelpiece, studying the photograph of Frannie's mother. 'It's that bad?'

'Yes.'

The farmer drew a deep breath. 'Eh now, trust me, trust thaself lad. It's gone wrong, but it's not thy fault. Now, I'll draw up documents for you and Tomas to let me act for you. You can witness each other's. I've been in business long enough for that. Leave 'em with me. I'll move 'em somewhere safe for tonight. What about money?'

'Money's not a problem. We've worked hard. And Tomas and I won't take anything with us,' Anthony said.

'Nowt?'

'Just a bit of cash to get us to the coast. We'll go back home, get rid of all our clothes, anything with our scent on it. We'll say our goodbyes here, on the farm. I'll feel better if I leave her with you, even if she can't stay for long.'

'Aye, I understand. I'll come up wi' some tale for t'village.' He paused. 'That lad of yours? Any idea yet?'

Anthony looked closely at his father-in-law. 'You want him to be ... like me. Don't you?' It was a new and startling concept for him.

Eddie paused for a moment, disconcerted, then laughed. 'Aye, it's true. I grew up wi' these tales from my grandad, about wolf people who used to live round here. T'idea of my grandson being one of 'em ... well, it tickles me. He's just a normal little lad though.'

Anthony nodded. 'We're all just normal kids until the first change. I hope and pray that I can get home before that happens, if it happens.'

'What will be will be,' his father-in-law said, nodding. 'Now, let's get back t'kitchen.'

Anthony found Tomas, Miriam and the children playing football in the farmyard. John was shouting enthusiastically. Anthony watched the two boys for a while, wondering how his cold-blooded calculation had led to these perfect, beautiful children, so loved and wanted. It didn't matter any more whether they were werewolf or half-blood. They were the next generation. John, good-natured, generous and affectionate almost to a fault, would need a cynical and sensible friend to help him through life. Mark was already showing signs of being that friend. As Anthony watched his son, the child looked up and smiled openly, trustingly. Anthony knelt as the boy ran towards him for the last time, drawing him to him, not daring to scare him by squeezing too tightly. 'I love you, Mark. You won't remember, but I do, and I always will,' Anthony whispered. The boy wriggled, uncomfortable, then freed himself from the embrace and stepped back. 'Play football,' he demanded. Anthony glanced through the kitchen window and saw Frances and Eddie deeply involved with the drafting of the documents that would be necessary. He decided that a few last minutes of happiness wouldn't betray anyone, and whispered to his son, 'You and me against Uncle Tomas and John?'

Mark's smile made everything worthwhile, and the next half-hour passed by too quickly. Eventually, Frannie called them all indoors, and the documents were signed. Frannie shifted uncomfortably, looking at Anthony. 'What next?' she asked him.

'You hide, we run and draw attention away from you. Both of you have to stay quiet, forever. You understand?' he glanced at Miriam, who nodded seriously.

'I understand. I've not been a perfect wife, but Tomas is my best friend, and he wouldn't lie to me. You can all trust me,' she said soberly. 'I guess this is where I really grow up,' she added dourly.

Anthony nodded, believing her. 'I guess this is where we all grow up. I'm sorry, all of you.'

Frannie shook her head. 'Don't be. Don't be sorry.' Her face was solemn, and her eyes shone. 'I never expected anyone like you. I still don't understand why you love me, but I know you do. Don't be sorry for any of it.'

Anthony brushed aside his instinctive shame. He had courted her at first for her half-blood, but he couldn't remember a time when the sight of her hadn't brightened his day. He struggled, as always, to find the right words. In the end, she said them for him.

'It's done, my love. If you really are going to leave, then the sooner the better, I think. It's time to say goodbye.'

'Now?' With the moment there, he was trapped, his legs were lifeless.

'Now, both of you. There's nothing to gain by staying here any longer, is there?'

'Oh Fran…' he whispered.

Mark had been watching them. 'Where's Daddy going?' he asked.

Anthony winced. 'A long way away, but it's a secret, can you keep a secret?' he said.

Mark nodded. 'I can keep secrets. Who will look after Mummy?'

Frances picked him up, smiling. 'We'll look after each other, my love. Won't we?'

'Yes.' Mark looked at her intently. He was still

looking at her when Anthony kissed him gently on the cheek, and then took his wife and son into his arms and kissed Frances for the last time, his eyes open, watching her, tasting her, loving her. Behind him, Tomas and Miriam were explaining things to John, who was beginning to cry.

Anthony drew away at last, backing away to the door. He called to Tomas, who hugged Miriam one last time, and joined him. 'Come on, brother,' Anthony murmured. Together they walked away from the farmhouse, away from the farm, and back to their homes. They spent an hour carefully destroying and burning anything that associated them with their families, including photographs, clothes and bedding with their scent on, letters, and diaries. At last, satisfied that they had done all they could, they walked away from their homes, taking the southward road to exile.

Chapter 22

Ramsgate seemed like a less obvious departure point than Dover, and the brothers made their way there by a complex route, arriving in Ramsgate four days after leaving Lancashire. They were certain they hadn't been followed, and were playing down their twinhood. Anthony had grown a full beard and moustache, and had cut his hair short. Tomas's curls were shoulder-length, and he was clean-shaven. They were obviously brothers, that couldn't be hidden. They'd picked up some extra cash, working a con in Norwich two nights earlier, which had paid for their tickets, new fake French passports and identity cards.

Miguel's murder had made the Manchester papers, but not the national ones. It had been reported as a random gang-related incident, the murder of a 'mystery man'. None of the killers had been caught, and there were no known suspects. Tomas was as distressed by the murder as he was about leaving his family. He'd met his older brother, and respected him. For Anthony, the murder was more abstract. Miguel had been a tale told at the dinner table, a hero he had never met – but still, a rage had been kindled and he made no effort to quench it.

Tomas had spotted the enemy before Anthony, and had casually made his way back to his brother. 'Just two of them, not twins, but close enough in looks that they could be if they were the same age. A man in his thirties, and another in his late teens. White hair, the older one is almost bald. Thick necks, solid guys, but not fat. Thick lips. Do we kill them now or later?'

Anthony blinked. 'They're trained soldiers...'

'So now? Before they recognise us and attack first?'

'So ... so we don't just rush in and try to kill two trained warriors. Especially not here. We don't do anything in England. It'll confirm our presence here, and so far they only suspect it. We need to think about it.'

Tomas scowled. Anthony cleared his throat. 'Look, that ferry doesn't have many places to hide, and we're more likely to be spotted together. You go now, I'll take the next one.'

'Leaving it two against one?' Tomas frowned.

'Only if they spot you, and they're not expecting us to be on board anyway...'

Tomas reluctantly agreed, and it was eight hours later that the brothers were reunited in Calais. Tomas was tight-lipped, and was wearing a long sweater that Anthony had not seen before.

'Why the change of clothes?' he asked.

'Blood on my shirt. Don't worry, nobody saw it. I did it when we disembarked.'

'Did what?' Anthony's stomach tightened.

'Got rid of them, easy enough, one at a time. I built up a lot of muscle building houses, enough to strangle one and put some real force into stabbing the other. With the knife the first one was carrying, which was nice.' Tomas's voice was flat. 'Come on, one body is in the water, I weighted it with the guy's own suitcase. The other is in a crate. It might not be found for months, or it might already be found. We need to move.'

'You killed? Two men?' Anthony swallowed.

'That's the general idea, isn't it?' Tomas gave a thin smile. 'Like I said, we need to move.'

They went back to the small farmhouse where they had grown up. It was now home to another family who had bought it from the twins' parents years ago. The new family were sympathetic and offered them a meal, but they didn't know anything about their parents or sisters.

Tomas and Anthony accepted the meal gratefully, and then made their way around the area, showing their faces in cafes and markets, sometimes recognised, sometimes not. Nobody knew where their parents and sisters had moved to, although many remembered them, and also remembered the blond twins who had arrived a few weeks earlier, introduced themselves as relatives, and asked about the family.

Eventually, in a village twenty miles away from the old farmhouse, their questions were answered by a middle-aged woman who said nothing, but led them to her home. In a back room, a once attractive young man, with unkempt blond curls and bright blue eyes, sat staring into space. 'My son, Andre,' the woman said, and left.

The son didn't speak for a long time, glancing

sneakily at them when he thought they were looking the other way, refusing to answer any of their gentle questions. Anthony and Tomas frowned, puzzled, not understanding why they had been led to this madman. Eventually, Andre stood and walked to Tomas, touching his long dark curls, gently tracing his finger around Tomas's eyes. Tomas submitted, puzzled but trusting that the madman meant no harm. Eventually, Andre spoke. 'Sylvia. Where is Sylvia?'

Anthony half rose from the seat, then subsided. 'We don't know, we hoped that you did. We are her brothers. Did she talk about us? Tomas and Anthony?'

Andre nodded. 'Tomas and Anthony. You look like her, pretty. She talked about you. She called the baby Anthony.'

The brothers exchanged a long look. 'The baby? Were you married? Where is the baby? Where is Sylvia?'

Andre shook his head, and fell silent again. Anthony looked around. The wall was filled with sketches, pictures of the village, still lifes of flowers and pets. There were no portraits, but there were empty spaces on the wall. He searched through drawers until he found pencils and a sketch pad. He handed them to Andre.

'You're an artist, aren't you? Can you draw a picture of baby Anthony for me? I've not seen him, and he's my nephew. Please?'

The madman shrugged, taking the pencil and paper, applying one to the other for several minutes,

Fight for the Future

pausing, amending the portrait slightly until he was happy with it, pausing again to sign it. He passed it to Anthony who moaned and closed his eyes. Tomas reached across to look at the picture, then turned away, leaving it face up on the table. The picture showed, in a few deft lines, a baby, not much more than a year old, dead in the road. The child had blond curls, and bore a strong resemblance to Andre. The death had been brutal. There was a blurred, indistinct shape next to the baby.

Anthony forced himself to speak. 'You saw this? You found your son like this? Where was Sylvia?'

'He wasn't dead until I picked him up. They'd broken his neck, but he didn't die until I moved him out of the dust.' Andre looked up, a brief moment of horrified clarity in his blue eyes. 'I killed my son.'

Tomas was there with him in seconds, holding him. 'No, don't think that. You didn't, you tried to save him. Who killed him Andre? Did you see the bastards?'

'I don't know. They killed her too. They killed her, I found her body with the baby's. I went to look for help. When we got back, her body was gone.'

Anthony's mouth was dry. He went to the kitchen, coming back with a jug of water and three glasses. When he could speak, he moved closer to Andre. 'Do you know what happened to Audrey? Did you know Sylvia's twin?'

Andre shook his head. 'I tried to find her, and you, and your mother and father. Everyone says they are dead too.'

Tomas looked up slowly, meeting Anthony's gaze. Anthony spoke again. 'Who says that?'

Andre shrugged. 'What are you going to do?'

'We're going to find out what happened to Audrey and our parents, then we're going to look for whoever killed your son. And we will get our revenge. Now, the sooner you tell us where to find someone who knows what happened to Audrey and our parents, the sooner I can start ripping large pieces off the people who killed Sylvia and your son.'

Tomas protested. 'Anthony!'

'Shut up. He's sat here for weeks, doing nothing. And now he's stalling us. Andre. Give me names, now.'

'You can't speak to me like that, I've been hurt.' Andre picked up the pencils again and began a sketch of Sylvia, her eyes closed, her mouth slack. Anthony hit the table. 'Names, now. Or I start with you, you worthless piece of shit. Where were you? Why weren't you injured? Why didn't you defend them?'

'I ran. We were out walking in the lanes. Four men came and attacked us. I ran. They let me. Are you happy now? Can I go back to forgetting again?' Andre looked at the table. Tomas pulled away, all sympathy gone. Anthony smiled thinly as Tomas spoke. 'You'd better give him those names, before we start ripping pieces off you.'

Andre shrugged. He wrote several names and addresses down. He pushed the paper across the table, and started to sketch again, pictures of a dead

Fight for the Future

child. Anthony took the paper and stood up. As he and Tomas left the room, their brother-in-law whispered. 'I want to die.' They ignored him.

Every one of the people they spoke to confirmed the story. In various ways they were all sure that the twins had been orphaned, that Audrey was dead too. Some had seen bodies, some had heard fighting. One elderly farmer, finally convinced that the twins were the sons of the dead couple, took them aside. 'I hid the bodies. I didn't know them well, but they were good people, you know? They were good to me. I had to hide their bodies, that's why it's been hard for you to find out. But I promise you that they were dead.'

'Why did you hide my parents' bodies?' asked Anthony, stony-faced. The old man shivered. 'Lycanthropy. You won't believe it, your generation doesn't, but werewolves exist. Your parents were killed by monsters, they were infected by their bites, their bodies were monstrous, twisted, inhuman. I couldn't let my friends be seen like that, in life or death. Nobody would believe it. I don't expect you to.'

Anthony nodded. He emptied his pockets, and Tomas did the same. They gave everything they owned to the old man, thanking him for his service to their parents. They returned to the village three days after they had left it. They passed Andre's mother, who was dressed in black. She made the sign of the evil eye at them, and spat at their feet. Anthony stopped. 'Your son?'

'He hung himself, when you left him. Are you

happy?' She echoed her son's question.

'No, we're not. It doesn't bring our sister back. And she found something to love in him, didn't she?' Tomas spoke quietly, soothingly. He didn't want this woman's hatred. In reply, she spat on his boots again. Anthony took his arm, and they walked out of town.

Alone, hungry, penniless, orphaned, they stood at the side of the road and considered their options.

'We need a city. We need to be somewhere where people meet, and talk, and do business. Our enemies can't survive without doing business with the outside world. We'll go to Paris.' Anthony spoke authoritatively. 'We'll track them down, and we'll kill as many as we can.'

Tomas shrugged. 'You talk about killing. You haven't yet struck a blow in anger. Violence is not easy, it changes you, even when you just want to teach some cocky wife-stealer a lesson, it changes you. Don't talk about it so easily, brother. You weren't the one who saw Miguel die.'

Chapter 23

They made their way slowly to Paris, living on the land, changing to hunt, working the occasional half-day for farmers. When they got to the city they had enough money to rent a small room. They cleaned it up, and began to get their faces known, and to learn their way around Paris. They tried to draw out the enemy, letting their names be known, the names they'd gone by before they arrived in England. They took care not to let others know where they lived, but were otherwise rash, even getting into conversations about werewolves and vampires. Nothing happened. They started to change, one at a time, to spend a few minutes in the early hours in wolf form, spraying their scent around the city. They were desperate for revenge, and Anthony sometimes wondered if they weren't seeking their own deaths as much as those of their enemies. He dreamed of Frances and Mark, and in every dream they were dead by the road while he ran away. He woke with their names on his lips.

One night, working a shift in a bar, he wondered if he should just get it all over with by putting an advertisement in the newspaper. 'Rogue werewolves seek fight with religious inbreds. Please reply to Box Number 87.' He was in a foul mood, and had been asked to lighten up several times by his employer. 'Hey, Anthony, we hired you because you're good-looking and charming, you bring the ladies in! Leave your personal problems at home and smile, eh?'

Anthony satisfied himself with one long glare

at the boss, then put on a professional face and started to chat to the customers. He disliked his job; he hated the cigarette smoke, the drunken punters and, most of all, he loathed the fact that he had learned everything he needed to know to do the job well on his first night. He could feel his life slipping away. He wasn't drawing out the Whites, and he wasn't doing anything at all to make Frances and Mark safer. It was a relief when a barrel needed to be changed, and he went downstairs to sort it out. When he got back, his twin was leaning against the other side of the bar, explaining to the boss that while he had no moral objection to pouring drinks for strangers, he would prefer to be paid for it. The boss was getting pissed off until he spotted Anthony climbing back into the bar. 'Oh, twins. I see, very funny.' Anthony shrugged. He could see this particular period of employment ending quickly and acrimoniously. He made a show of looking around for customers before nodding to the boss and leaning across the bar to speak to his brother. 'Buy a bloody drink, or I get the sack,' he muttered. Tomas pushed some cash across the bar. 'Get one yourself. I've got news,' he said, smiling broadly.

'Something to get our teeth into?' Anthony sounded hopeful.

'Perhaps, in a good way. Do you remember me marking that corner near the Champs-Élysées last week? You told me it was pointless, because humans piss on it all the time...'

Anthony grinned. 'Yeah, you got seen and I had to pretend that you were my dog.'

'Yes, well. I got a reply.' Tomas's smile was getting broader by the minute.

'How many?' Anthony asked.

'One. She's alone.' Tomas looked at him, waiting eagerly for the response.

'She?' Anthony licked his upper lip. 'You sure?'

'Young, female and, if I remember Mama's scent well, fertile as fuck.'

'And?' Anthony leaned across the bar, whispering now.

Tomas looked at him, smiling nervously now, puzzled by Anthony's reaction.

'And ... get your arse over this side of the bar, we're going to track her down.'

Anthony shrugged. 'No. It's pointless. We don't want a mate. We're married, we've got kids.'

Tomas rolled his eyes. 'Miriam won't be waiting for me, I'm sure of that.'

His brother shook his head. 'That's not all. What are you going to do with this hypothetical female? Is she alone? Does she want to meet you?'

'Anthony, she pissed on my mark. That's a come-on, isn't it?'

'Don't. Just don't. It complicates things. What are you thinking of? A nice little cottage with a white fence and roses, and two dozen little werewolves running around?'

Tomas smiled smugly. 'Australia. We'll take her to Australia. We'll be safe there.'

'We? What *we*? Tomas, we can't afford a pack, it's too dangerous. It's not what we planned! What happened to revenge? To protecting our families? And how do you expect to get to Australia? And I'm not interested, if I can't have Frannie...'

'Yeah, yeah, yeah. I get it, you've got principles. But check her out with me, we don't have to take things further.' Tomas put on his most appealing expression, making his dark-brown eyes wide and innocent.

Anthony bit his lip. He was curious to see this stranger, to meet another werewolf. He finally agreed to go, after work. 'But I'm not interested. OK?' he insisted.

Anthony was unprepared for his reaction. He'd changed to his wolf form in a quiet alley, and allowed Tomas to lead him to the corner. His first experience of the scent of an unrelated female hit him like a truck. Even covered by traffic smells and the traces of human piss, he could pick up her scent. It called to him, to every cell of him, and he knew that he wanted her, desperately and completely. He whined and scratched, sniffing around for a trail, a scent to follow, to find her. He was abruptly conscious of being scruffed and dragged away by Tomas. He growled threateningly, but Tomas laughed and drew him underneath a railway arch. Anthony changed back, and Tomas passed him his clothes.

Anthony's eyes were still flashing yellow, but he was calming down. 'Fuck. How the hell do packs function when the girls smell like that?'

Tomas shrugged. 'I know, I guess you just get used to it.'

Fight for the Future

'How? Oh hell, she smells so good.' He turned, unthinking, towards the place where the female had made her mark. He closed his eyes, and shuddered. 'Why didn't we know about her years ago?' he said quietly.

His twin wasn't looking at him. He answered him vaguely. 'Oh, maybe she's young, not pack-born. You know what Mama used to tell us – the half-bloods have werewolf young now and again. Maybe this girl doesn't know what the hell is happening to her. We could teach her, look after her.'

Anthony finished buttoning his shirt. 'No. At the very most, we speak to her and tell her the situation, tell her that she's not alone, and clue her into the White Pack problem. But she's not joining us. It's too late, we can't afford to look after her. You've smelled her, she'd be irresistible. How do we go on the attack with a mate and babies to look after? And, more to the point, I've made promises. I'm not available, you understand?'

Tomas laughed uneasily. 'We're not talking about some floozy getting between you and your marriage vows – this woman is one of us. When we got married, we never anticipated this.'

His brother shook his head. 'I considered it, and we've talked about it before, you know we have. It's not going to happen, Tomas. She gets a quick history lesson, at the very most, then we leave.'

'But we could hide her away somewhere.'

'And then how do we support her? How do we hide a pack? Our parents spent their entire lives hiding, hiding kids, banishing us as soon as we could pass for adults and earn our own living. Twins attract attention, multiple sets of twins will always be talked about, and the Whites are constantly alert for that kind of gossip. The best we can do is damage the White Pack enough to make the world a safer place in the future. That's our job, Tomas, we've talked about this. We're taking Miguel's place.'

Tomas leaned against the wall, his arms crossed, his face dark and brooding. 'You think I'm forgetting Miriam and John? I'm not. I'm not stupid – whatever happens with this wolf woman, I'll never speak a word about them. I'll protect them to the day I die. But I don't think I can let this chance go. It would be a real life, like we're supposed to have. I'll take her to America, or Australia.'

'Wherever, they'll find you. You'd really leave me alone, Tomas? Is that what you're saying?'

'No, of course not. Come with us, we could see if we could make it work with three of us. It shouldn't be a problem.'

'Tomas, I'm saying no. I'm saying that it's a very bad idea. We can't leave her alone and clueless, I admit that, but I'm having nothing more to do with her.' He looked at his brother, at the disappointment in his face. 'All right, we'll meet her, talk about things. We're making a lot of assumptions here. Maybe she's already in a pack, maybe she's inviting us to join an existing set up. But first, we'll get some sleep. It's late, and I'm tired.'

Tomas agreed, and they made their way, by a serpentine route, to their room.

Two hours later, Anthony awoke, troubled. Something was wrong. He listened for the sound that had disturbed him, and realised that there was nothing. It was the nothing that had woken him – he couldn't hear the regular sound of Tomas's breathing in the other bed. He slipped quietly out of bed and looked around, glancing out of the window. He couldn't see his twin. He had no choice, no other way to find his brother, so he changed, there, in the room, and jumped gracefully out of the first-floor window, his strong legs taking the impact of his fall. He cast around for Tomas's scent, finding, to his relief, the human scent of him. Tomas was heading straight for the Champs-Élysées, and the mark made by the female werewolf.

Anthony didn't waste time following the scent trail. He simply ran as fast as he could towards his brother's intended destination. At the fateful corner, he could smell his own mark, Tomas's over it, and the female's over that. Tomas had returned, and so had she. Perhaps she'd been waiting, watching for them. Keeping to the shadows, he tracked her wolf scent to underneath the same bridge that he and Tomas had hidden beneath. Where the wolf scent ended, a new scent started, a human female. Anthony stood for a while, unsure, cursing his lack of experience in these matters. Finally, he decided to track the woman, rather than Tomas. He was reasonably sure that they would have found each other by now. Sure enough, three streets away, the scent of the woman was joined by his brother's scent, overlaying it. Within another couple of streets, the scents were side by side. Tomas had caught up with her here and they had stood for a while. The scents were strong, equally fresh, and led away from the centre of the city. There was no attempt to hide; the pair were walking in the middle of the pavement with a destination clearly in mind. Anthony recognised the excitement in his brother's scent. The female's scent carried an undercurrent of fear. Anthony explained it as nervousness; Tomas was a strong, well-built, fast, excitable man, and a woman alone with him at night might be a little nervous.

Anthony whined, scared. He was making his way uphill, along a wide open city street, the only cover shop doorways. He slipped from one to the next, aware that soon the morning people would be out, the cleaners and delivery drivers. Already, lights in flats above the shops were coming on. The city was waking up.

In one shop doorway, he realised that the couple had also stopped there. Anthony growled angrily, jealousy and fear making his whole body vibrate. It was happening, what he had feared. The couple had stopped here, their scents were strong, and changing. They must, at last, have surrendered to their instincts, surrendered to that first kiss that started the bonding process. The black wolf had, for a moment, an image of how he'd wanted the meeting to go: in public, with both twins meeting the woman in a situation where they had to behave with some decorum, where they could have met her, and spoken to her, and gracefully withdrawn. In the dark, alone, in the excitement of their first encounter with a potential mate, Tomas and the woman had been helpless. The wolf wondered, enviously, if she was beautiful, if she was charming and intelligent and brave. He remembered his Frances, and kept that memory in his mind as he followed the mixed trail. His brother's scent, that he had known so intimately since their first change, was different. New chemicals were being formed in Tomas's cells, a response and a challenge to the female with him. A mutual addiction was being created, and Anthony could only follow helplessly, anxiously. Tomas was becoming a First.

Anthony guessed that he was no more than ten minutes behind the pair now. He was walking steeply uphill, towards Père Lachaise Cemetery, the Parisian city of the dead. Pausing occasionally to check the scent trail, he found himself at the main gate. The pair seemed to have walked straight through it. Baffled, he cast around, but the gate was closed, and the trail went straight through it. Now, unsettled, he tried to work out the puzzle. His wolf brain hurt, and he sought his human form, needing that intelligence.

Naked by the cemetery gates, he stood, trembling. Somehow, the gates had been opened, and they were now closed. He knew without thinking about it that Tomas, blinded by the bonding process, would have barely noticed the incongruity of open gates at this hour. So who had opened them, and who had closed them again? Terrified now, Anthony fell instinctively back into his wolf form and ran fast and low beside the walls, casting around for a way into the cemetery. Four hundred yards past the gate, he could hear low voices – Tomas and a woman. She was protesting, he was puzzled and soothing. It was clear to Anthony that she was trying to back away, to stop the bonding before it was completed. There was a real fear in her voice. Why would she fear it, when she'd gone to such lengths to attract them, to bring Tomas to her? Anthony fought against panic, and raced further around the cemetery, at last finding a section of wall that was low enough and clear enough for him to leap, to gain a purchase, to scramble upwards and crouch silently, looking down into the city of the dead, the narrow footpaths between graves, the wide streets between the mausoleums. A small, cautious movement caught his eye, a wide-eyed black cat was staring at him in fear. He looked away deliberately, and the creature ran into the shadows, grateful for its life.

He crawled along, just inside the wall, low to the ground and reluctant to reveal himself. Turning a corner, hidden by undergrowth, he finally saw his brother sitting on a gravestone, holding the hand of a slim, pale-eyed, dark-haired woman. A breeze caught her scent and brought it to him, and he closed his eyes, savouring it for a moment, an illicit pleasure. With all his attention on his sense of smell, he realised that the breeze was bringing another unfamiliar smell – male, related to that of the female. His eyes snapped open, and he peered into the darkness. He saw, barely thirty yards away from Tomas, pale shapes among the graves. Men, intent on the scene in front of them, intent on the sight of Tomas reassuring the woman, touching her gently, soothing her fear. He misunderstood her terror. Anthony did not. He shot from the shadows, a dark line of fury moving towards the girl, growling deep and loud.

Tomas saw the movement, and moved to defend the woman, but not fast enough. She was knocked off her feet and into the gravestone behind her. She lay stunned, bleeding. Tomas turned to his brother. 'Jealous? How could you...' He trailed off, as eight pure-white wolves emerged confidently from the shadows. A grinning man led them. Tomas swallowed, looked around. The bleeding girl was dark-haired, but as she lay on the ground, highlighted by the moonlight, a thin strand of white hair shone bright. Tomas bowed his head in recognition and resignation. He touched Anthony's head once, in benediction.

'I choose Miguel's way. Go, brother, and avenge us. I love you. When you next see John, be his father, for me.' His whisper carried no further than Anthony's ears. Understanding, but hating himself, Anthony turned and ran for the wall. He heard the sound of ripping fabric as Tomas threw himself into the change. He heard screams and howls and growls. He heard the sound of flesh hitting stone, and dying moans. Tomas was still alive, Anthony recognised his growls. He recognised his screams of pain. He reached the wall, and scrambled up, halted by teeth at his tail. He whipped it out of the way, and turned around, just in time to take his assailant by the throat. He braced himself, the whole weight of his enemy suspended from his jaws. Every sinew in his body resisted the fall back into the cemetery and he bit down, the fresh exciting forbidden taste of wolf blood in his throat hitting him like a drug. The dead White fell away, and Anthony took one last look into the cemetery. The leader was still human. He was bent over the woman.

'Ruined, half mated. Stupid creature,' the blond commented. The woman raised her head. 'Harald, brother, I did as you said.'

'Yes, good work, little sister,' the man said, before slitting her throat in one easy, practised movement and striding to the moiling mass of fur around Tomas. Anthony shuddered again as the blond looked up, straight at him. The man laughed. 'You next, mongrel bastard. Wait there, I'll take you myself.' Anthony whined, torn between Tomas's wish, and his overwhelming desire to throw himself into the fight. Intelligence, and the cold wish for vengeance, won. Here lay certain death. The future was his to fight for. He took one last look at the scene. Three of the Whites lay dead, another two were dying. Three more were squabbling over the remains of something red and wet and torn. Anthony stored the picture in his heart, and looked deep into the eyes of his enemy. Harald took a step back, unnerved, then laughed uneasily.

The black wolf leaped back into the city of the living, and ran away from danger, away from the horror of his twin's death. Anthony retreated deep into the mind of the wolf, away from the grief that threatened to destroy him. Somewhere between the cemetery and the countryside, he sealed his agony

Fight for the Future

and intelligence into a bleak cell in his mind, leaving only the desire for vengeance and the knowledge, at last, of who his enemy was.

Chapter 24

The enemy was close behind him, he was outnumbered, and every one of them matched him in strength.

And now he was in the middle of a city, in wolf form, as dawn broke and the citizens started to leave their homes and go about their business. He knew that the White Pack soldiers would follow Harald's orders and take risks that Anthony could ill afford to. He gambled that they would be tired after the battle, and hopefully wounded. His only chance lay in putting as much distance between him and them as possible.

He ran, pure and fast, using the widest, busiest roads. He held little hope that the crush of people and stink of traffic would mask his scent, but he knew he couldn't waste time skulking in gardens and looking for shelter. He wouldn't survive the day with that tactic. He tore along the pavement, running as he'd never run before. He blanked out the reasons why he was running, and only allowed himself to know that he was escaping mortal danger.

People scattered as he approached, car horns blared and, behind him, he heard the sound of sirens. He took a chance and ducked up a side street, then turned again and continued in the same direction, on a slightly less busy street. He heard the faint howls of the White Pack behind him and considered that, in Harald's place, he would put a silent runner ahead of the main hunters, to deceive the victim as to the Pack's location. He increased his speed, aware of

Fight for the Future

everything around him. A woman screamed as she stumbled out of his way, a cyclist came to an amazed stop right in his path, and Anthony leaped high over him, landing without a stumble on the smooth, hard pavement. He felt a sharp pain in his paw, probably a broken bone, but he pushed it to the back of his mind and continued at the same pace. He was trackable, he knew. He needed to break the trail, but swimming or wading down a stream or river was a poor tactic with multiple pursuers who could investigate a long length of bank to find his exit point.

The avenue he was on intersected with a busy main road. His sense of smell was almost overcome by a jumble of new and interesting scents, and he realised he was close to the zoo, and the surrounding woodlands. He was tempted; they looked safe, he could den there, and find food. It was the obvious place to lie low for the day. He paused and looked around. People were staring at him. He gathered himself up, watched the traffic, and jumped on to the bed of the next truck that went past. As traffic slowed, he leaped on to another lorry going in the other direction. He crouched down and watched through the slats at the back as four white wolves tore round the corner, fast on his trail. They overshot, running across the road and heading for the zoo. The last he saw of them, they were casting around for his trail. The sound of sirens got louder, and he forgot his troubles and laughed as police cars converged on the small pack of wolves that stood, furious, just outside the zoo.

Six hours later, the lorry came to a final halt on the outskirts of Le Mans. Anthony had slept, and was hungry. He couldn't let anyone spot him; rumours of a large black wolf would get back to the White Pack very fast. He wondered if Harald and his soldiers had escaped, and decided to act on the assumption that they had. He leaped out of the lorry and skulked away, looking for a place to eat and heal.

He knew he was remarkable. Half as big again as the biggest European wolves, he would raise questions wherever he was seen. He would be safer, and more anonymous, in human form. The thought of his human shape reminded him of all he had lost, and he pulled away sharply from the idea. He would hide, and make his plans, and remain lupine.

As the months passed, he made his way south to the Pyrenees, finding and trailing a small pack of Iberian wolves who had escaped Franco's slaughter. The female leader of the pack was aware of him, and feared him at first. His size and intelligence gave him an advantage, and he deliberately hunted wild boar, leaving his kills for the pack. He never attempted to join them or hunt with them, but his gifts made an impression, and they tolerated him hanging around. His association with the pack made it less likely that his presence in the hills would be the subject of conversation among humans. He was just another wolf. Nevertheless, he avoided people as much as he could. He rolled on the ground where the pack had rested, mixing their scent with his own. He pissed in running water whenever he could, and buried his scat. He began to forget how to be human, and as time passed he knew only that he had to kill the white wolf.

When spring came he started to move east, following the mountains until he reached the coast, and then moving north towards the Italian Alps. There was plenty of prey, and he'd learned how to stay hidden. He covered his scent, while casting around for signs of White Pack wolves. As he crossed into Switzerland, he found an old camp. Harald had been human there, less than two months ago. There had been ten men there altogether, all brothers. Any trail was old, and hard to follow, but he was patient and looked for signs of human and wolf scat in the same place, and of raw and cooked bones in the same midden. The group was travelling in both human and wolf form, combining the benefits of each, setting human and wolfen guards over their camp while some of the group took what rest they needed. They had a goal in mind, they were moving steadily towards something, their journey a calm progression. They weren't being chased. And they didn't know that they were being followed.

In Bavaria, he saw, and was seen by, a blond child with White Pack features. The child fled, and Anthony followed carefully. He came to the outskirts of a village, and watched from the shadows as the people went about their lives. The population was white, Germanic, and overwhelmingly blonde, but they weren't werewolves. Some of them had the White Pack look about them, and Anthony realised that they were descendants of the Pack, normal or half-blood, tolerated because of their strong resemblance to the Pack. He listened, forcing his brain down long-disused human pathways, and was startled when Harald's name was mentioned by a teenager buying supplies from a market stall.

'Harald's leaving again, I hear. He's only been back on the mountain for a few weeks, but Gunther doesn't want him around and is sending him out to hunt that last mongrel.'

The trader shrugged. 'Mountain politics doesn't bother me, as long as you people come down to buy and sell on time and fairly, I don't care what's going on.'

The teenager scowled. He was White Pack, without a doubt. Anthony suppressed a growl, and watched as the boy left and headed into a road that curved into a forested slope.

Anthony glanced upwards and to his left, at a wooded mountain that rose gradually from the valley. Anthony swallowed, and started to creep backwards into the undergrowth. He had found the home of his enemy, and it was clear that he was dealing with a force bigger than he'd ever imagined.

A woman approached the trader, looking anxious. 'My lad just got home, he says he surprised a big wolf, a couple of miles out of town. Nothing weird about that, you know the wolves round here don't hurt us, but ⋯ he said this one was pure black. I thought I'd better warn people. Just be careful⋯'

She continued on her way, spreading news

Fight for the Future

that Anthony very much wanted to stop. The trader shrugged. 'Probably a bear, all the wolves round here are white. The kid must have seen something big and thought wolf.'

It was time to leave. He knew where the White Pack lived, and that was very interesting information.

Two scouts encountered him, ten miles south. They were young soldiers who had been taught that they were the elite, born to victory. Anthony fought dirty and ate their hearts and livers when he'd done with them. He ran for thirty hours, a slow, steady lope, stopping only to drink, or to piss in running water. He stayed away from roads, knowing that the Whites would have access to vehicles and the means to overtake him. He couldn't keep the pace up, and began to take rest breaks, to hide and find some sleep. When prey was hard to find, he visited human settlements and stole whatever he could from empty houses. Staying unseen was vital, but he had to eat.

He found wolf scat, just three wolves, heading north, and took time to reverse the roles and hunt them down. They were on their way back to their mountain, and hadn't heard that he was around. He approached the camp, skirting the wolf guard, and killed the sleeping Pack member quickly and quietly, suffocating him with his jaws, careful not to break the skin and release the smell of blood. The guard taking human form was armed and following every procedure, but he clearly didn't believe that danger was possible. He went down hard, and the end was bloody. Anthony was stabbed in the thigh of a back leg, and lost blood of his own. The third soldier was ready for him, and in wolf form. He was a true opponent, and the fight was long, noisy and bloody. Anthony left his enemy dying in the snow, and limped away to put distance between them. He decided not to provoke any more fights. It was time to hide again. Those months in the Pyrenees seemed idyllic now, and he stumbled south, healing slowly, scavenging, aware that he needed to heal, but that there was nowhere to hide. Weeks had passed, and he realised that every White Pack soldier must now know his scent. And there were hundreds of them.

A stroke of luck brought him to a bend in a river where a spit of sand led to an island. A storm was coming, and Anthony crossed the sandbar, and denned in a hollow tree. The summer downpour raised the river level and washed away his trail for miles upstream. He stayed on the island for three weeks, hunting fish, birds and small mammals. He left when he felt fully healed and rested, and continued his journey.

He was struggling now to remember a time without this thirst for vengeance. Harald had killed Anthony's twin and had to pay. But Harald had an army, and Anthony had nothing. He had vague memories of human form and a comfortable life, but they seemed like a dream. All he had was the journey, and the conflicting desires to hide, and to kill.

The fugitive evaded three White Pack groups as he crossed into Switzerland, and had a week or two with the sense that he was under no threat. Then he started to hear the howling of wolf patrols in the Italian Alps; the Whites had realised he had travelled faster and further than they'd expected, and had sent advance troops to intercept him.

He avoided the passes, keeping to the high forests, out of sight. Hunting was harder, and he started to lose weight. He scavenged the remains of a deer carcass from a wild wolf pack. They backed down at the sight of him. They were evidently familiar with wolves of his size, and were nervous.

The Pyrenees reared up before him, at last. He had hoped they would be a refuge, but the howling wolves were closing in, every night closer, several groups to the north and south and east of him. He lay down to sleep one night, under a rocky overhang near a wide meadow, and considered his situation. All he knew was that he had to kill the white wolf named Harald, and if other white wolves died, he didn't care. He no longer remembered why, but he knew it was kill or be killed. Harald and his brothers wouldn't stop until they knew that Anthony was dead. Running and hiding was no longer an option, he would have to make his stand.

The next day he studied the high bank of the meadow, where a steep drop-off fell to a fast-flowing river. He backtracked, studying the riverbanks upstream. He made no attempt to hide his tracks. He drank his fill where the stream was young, and set off back downstream. Excited howling behind him told him that his enemies had found his fresh trail. Then there was silence. He continued, loping now, an easy pace that he could keep up for hours. A different howling, one that he recognised. Harald had taken up the chase, and was moving closer. Harald wouldn't leave this to a subordinate group, he would take the glory for himself alone.

Anthony returned at last to the sunlit meadow where he'd decided that the end must come. He lay in the long grass, perfectly quiet. He listened and watched as six wolves entered the meadow. His heart sank; they were each a match for him. It took seconds for them to establish that he'd doubled back several times, and that he must be close by. He sighed, and stood, walking towards them. The leader growled, and the rest of the wolves fell back.

The two wolves approached each other, circling around each other. Anthony saw no physical weakness in this opponent. Without warning, he sprang forwards, going low, getting a mouthful of chest fur as Harald stepped back quickly, uninjured. Anthony regained his balance and was ready when Harald ran in equally low, aiming for the belly, then raising his jaws to scrape along Anthony's throat, drawing first blood, just a trickle. Anthony had hold of Harald's ear, and left a long tear in it as the white wolf withdrew and considered the situation. He nodded, a human gesture that Anthony recognised, then raised a paw. The other wolves started to move in. Harald wasn't going to take a risk against a strong opponent, and Anthony was not going to get a fair fight. The next few seconds were a blur of pain and claws and teeth, and it was only sheer momentum that took the rolling mass of bodies to the edge of the cliff.

As Anthony's consciousness faded, he felt the unstable ground beneath him crumble. The jaws that had fastened on to him loosened and left him free to fall and fall and fall.

Chapter 25

Six white wolves peered over the high bank of the river, watching as a sodden mass of dark fur swept downstream, unresisting, battered by the rocks, trailing blood. They watched until the body was out of sight, and then backed away from the treacherously slippery earth on to firmer ground.

Five of them whined nervously, unsure, while the sixth lay down in a patch of sunlight and started to lick carefully at a small bite wound on his left foreleg until he was satisfied with the results. Only then did he look at his companions. They were, of course, watching him attentively. He stood and stretched, enjoying the play of relaxation and tension in his muscles. Returning to the edge of the bank, he cocked his leg, and sent an arc of piss into the rushing water below.

Back on safe ground, he closed his eyes. His muscles began to writhe, his bones to deform and change, his fur was absorbed. When he opened his eyes again, he was a man – strong, with a tendency to heaviness. He had thin, white-blond receding hair, pale-blue eyes, and dark, fleshy lips. His five brothers changed to human form. They all looked remarkably similar.

The leader spoke. 'That's the last of them. Anthony Aubin is dead. We've succeeded, it's time to return home. Father believed that we would fail, like so many before us. We did not fail, and I expect great rewards when we return.'

Harald licked his lips and grinned. 'Home

then. We have done well.' With a last feral grin he melted quickly into wolf shape, forcing back his body's protest at the lack of recovery time since the last change. He watched with pleasure as his brothers demanded the same rigour of themselves, and transformed back into wolves.

When they were done, they rested, gathering their energy. The big white wolf threw his head back and howled his triumph three times, the sound carrying downriver on the water to where a bedraggled and bloody mess lay washed up on the sharp stones of the opposite bank.

Anthony's consciousness was a tiny hot flame of hate and will. His body was torn, but he still had a vestige of hearing left, and Harald's howling fanned the flame enough for him to get his bearings and take an inventory of his injuries. He was lying in cold, shallow water, on sharp rocks. He tried to move, but his legs were broken in several places. His eyes were whole and uninjured, but the flesh around them was swollen, blinding him. His muzzle was torn, a screaming flare of sensitive nerve endings. A sick numb feeling between his back legs worried him the most; he couldn't feel his balls, and hoped fervently that they were merely injured, and not detached completely. He knew he had shallow wounds on his belly, but he was fairly sure his innards were safe, and that the ugly pain from his liver and kidneys signalled nothing worse than bruising. So much for his body. He began to draw together information about recent events, but flinched away from the avalanche of memories. They were too painful, and he shut down again, drawing his resources back into that tiny, unthinking flame.

Later, it was cool, dark. He was awoken by a sharp pain close to his eye, and the sudden dry acrid taste of feathers in his mouth. A magpie had spotted him, and decided to dine on his eyes. Anthony's instincts had saved him, his head jerking up to grab the bird's wing. The creature was shrieking in fury, jabbing at him with its vicious beak. Anthony did not dare let go, he knew he would never get a better hold. He clamped his jaw down, feeling tiny bones crunch, and fell into blackness again. When he awoke, it was dark, the bird was weak, unresisting, but he sensed that it was still capable of escape. He hated the taste of feathers, but kept his mouth firmly shut. His legs were trapped beneath him and he rolled, to give them room to straighten. Now he needed to hold his head up a little, to keep it out of the inch or so of cold water that he was still lying in. All the separate pains had joined up, and his body was one throbbing agony. Anthony concentrated on the sound of the water around him, the rhythms of its movement. He could hear wind in the trees, then the sound of rain. He groaned. The last thing he needed was for the river level to rise. He knew he couldn't move yet. The bird was dying, but not fast enough. He waited for several minutes, gauging the rain. It was getting harder and faster; he couldn't wait any longer. He risked everything on one quick movement, releasing the magpie's wing and grabbing for the body. He almost missed, the bird had started to pull away from him as soon as his jaws had started to move, but it too was waterlogged and cold. Within seconds the bird – feathers, beak, feet and all – was just food in his stomach. He fought down the urge to vomit, and wondered how he was going to get out of the river. He healed fast, he knew that, and he tried to push against the shifting rocks of the river bottom. The pain was sudden, punishing, and intense, and he gasped, fainting again.

When he woke, he could barely feel his body. He knew that the next time he slept would be the last. The water level had risen, and he'd woken instinctively to raise his muzzle to save himself from drowning. He realised that he would soon be carried downstream again. He raised his head as far as possible, still blinded by the bruised, swollen flesh around his eyes. The sound of the water and the rain on the leaves told him where the shore was. He dipped his head again and drank, feeling the cold water hit his now-empty stomach. He tested his legs again, finding to his relief that he had regained some strength. He managed to drag himself a little further towards shore, the sharp stones lacerating him as he moved. He could smell his own blood in the water. He remembered the thick smell of Tomas's blood, the sight of Tomas's body scattered over ancient graves. Harald, bloody-faced, laughing.

His hatred and fury gave him a sudden strength, and he pushed again, raising his body out of the stream, crawling to the low muddy bank and throwing himself under the limited shelter of the trees. He decided to live. Tomas would be avenged.

Chapter 26

A week of hard travel brought Harald's group to the edge of their homeland. At the border, a low building served as a staging post for returning scouts and soldiers to dress and resupply. The brothers became human, fumbling with clumsy fingers at buttons and bootlaces. In human shape, Harald led his group to a fortified wall close to a high cliff. The door was opened for them without question, and they filed in. Harald looked hungrily to the left, at a blank stone wall that had hidden half of the Pack away from him for the last four decades. To his right, doors led to public and private rooms, including the room he had shared with his twin since they had come of age. Further in, a guarded door led to the quarters of the older women, those whom time had relieved from childbearing, and released to other duties. Harald grinned as he passed the door, remembering some of the duties he had imposed on these women in the past.

At the end of the corridor was a low, narrow doorway, the thick oak door closed against him. A guard attempted to meet Harald's glare, then blinked and looked over his shoulder, refusing to submit, but unable to meet the challenge. The guard spoke quietly and quickly.

'Gunther is busy. He will see you in one hour. He will hear your report then. He will, of course, be the first to hear it.'

Harald nodded, the father's wish, as always, a command. He turned to his fellows. 'Come, we'll wait in my room.' Once there, they relaxed fully for the first time in months. They spoke quietly about their triumphs, laughing as they recalled the deaths of certain enemies. At last, a sharp rap on the door told them that they were summoned, and they made their way to the Great Hall of the White Pack.

One by one, they passed through the narrow doorway, their eyes adjusting to the darkness within. Harald remembered the layout of the hall and started to walk confidently towards the back. As his vision adjusted, he saw guards standing formally behind a dark shadowed shape. As his eyes adjusted further, he recognised the First's chair, and his father seated there. He dropped to one knee and bowed his head. The calming, dominating essence of the pack leader, which he'd been unconsciously aware of since he'd entered the building, was now overpowering, and he found himself anxious to please the source of that power.

Gunther raised his hand. 'Report,' he ordered.

Harald raised his head. 'Success, Father. The whole pack of renegades and mongrels is dead.'

'Then let us give thanks to the gods for giving us the strength to maintain the purity of our line.' The older man spoke with a simple sincerity, and bowed his head in prayer. The guards followed suit and Harald, after a short pause, complied. He could hear his brothers behind him, mumbling the prayer.

At last the old man raised his head, and beckoned to Harald. 'You've done well. For generations that family has eluded us, hiding and running, interbreeding with the humans, joining the human community. That abomination is now gone. The six of you shall be rewarded. All of you are granted six months of leisure. For the rest of your lives, you may hunt my lands at will. Your access to the barren women is henceforth unrestricted. I am proud of you, and what you have done. Harald, my most favoured son, I also grant you access for one month to the mothers of our Pack.'

Harald bowed. It was, at once, more than he'd hoped for, and less than he knew he deserved. Gunther was clever; he knew that by setting Harald apart from the other five, he would sever him from their sympathy. It had been twenty years since Gunther had granted access to the Pack mothers to anyone else. Harald lowered his head in assent. 'I am grateful,' he said.

'Stay, tell me the tale. Guards, leave me, give orders for a feast. Harald will take the place of honour. The rest of you may leave. Sit, tell me everything,' Gunther said.

It took hours, and there were frequent questions. Eventually, the smell of roasting meat drew them to their feet, and out into a private corridor. To the left, it led across the back of the hall. Gunther smiled, gesturing. 'My quarters are back there, close to where the mothers make their home. Now, to the right, I have my own route to the dining room.' They walked for a few minutes, reaching a guard who bowed to them, and then opened a door and ushered them through. Harald stood for a moment, lit by the light of a hundred torches. Then the cheers started. He could feel the Alpha's hand on his shoulder, and he stood, enjoying the adulation. He let his father guide him to a chair at the high table.

As the night wore on, his distraction became more obvious. Eventually, Gunther made his excuses and led Harald back along the corridor to the mothers' quarters. The door stood open and, as the men walked in, silence fell across the large room. Harald had vague childhood memories of the scent and the sound and the look of this place. A huge central room was subdivided by tapestries and screens, sound was muffled by rugs and cushions, and comfortable chairs and sofas were filled with women of childbearing age, and older girls. The children were absent. Clearly they must be in the nurseries that led off from the central room. Empty dormitories filled with low bunks were visible.

So much he saw with his first swift glance. He was distracted by a brisk clapping noise to his left. He looked around, recognising Clara, the First female, and the only woman in the Pack with any rank at all, so far as he was concerned.

The younger girls were standing, picking up their sewing or weaving and making their way to one of the dormitories. A couple of them looked back at him with frank curiosity, but then the door was shut, and his attention returned to the mothers. He was surprised to realise that only a couple of them were pregnant, but stayed silent, glancing back at his father, who started to speak, quietly and soothingly.

'Mothers of the Pack, this is Harald. He has

led us to a great victory, he has brought to an end the mongrel pack, that offence to the gods. He will be visiting you for the next month. Please make him welcome, treat him as you would treat me.' He turned to leave, then paused. 'Clara, will you join me tonight?'

The old woman smiled with genuine affection, and took her mate's arm, going with him to their quarters. Harald was left with the women. He looked around, suddenly at a loss. They were all looking at him with varying degrees of interest. Eventually, when they seemed sure that Gunther was out of earshot, one of the obviously pregnant women stood and came to him.

'I'm Julia. I understand this is a privilege for you. For us, it may also be a joy. Gunther is ageing, and children are few. Will you allow me to make some suggestions?' She looked at him cautiously, and Harald abruptly realised that there must be some communication between the mothers and the older women who knew him. His name, and his reputation, would be familiar to them. In a way, that was good; these women would not expect him to be pleasant, or gentle.

'Speak, but remember who I am,' he said, not looking at her.

'Very well. We know our own bodies, we know who is most likely to conceive a child. If that is what you want—'

'Of course,' he snapped. 'As many as possible. I may only have a month to make my mark on the Pack.'

Fight for the Future

The woman's mouth twitched, and he realised she was suppressing a smile. She seemed to like him, and he found that puzzling. She looked around the room. Some of the women were trying to hide their distaste for this newcomer, others were looking at him with something akin to hope. She started to speak, but he interrupted, remembering something. 'I took a prisoner, months ago, is she here? A dark-haired woman, but she had a blond child.'

Julia paused, off balance. 'Audrey? The mongrel? She's a prisoner.' She spoke dismissively.

'Then I'll find her cell,' Harald said, with a faraway smile. 'Her brothers killed my brothers, and she needs to make amends for that. Now, Julia, if I'm going to breathe some new life into this pack, does it happen here?'

Julia's eyes widened, and she smiled at him again. 'Oh no, there is a private room. I'll take you there. We will come to you. Is that satisfactory?'

'Very.'

She led him to a pleasant, well-lit bedroom in a corner of the complex. Before she left, she paused. 'Harald? May I speak?'

'Briefly,' he said, already beginning to undress.

'I do find you interesting...'

He looked at her, amused. 'No, you seek power through me. Leave. Send your sisters to me.'

She left the room, annoyed. Her sisters looked up as she came out. 'He's ready, the pig,' she announced, watching as a woman in her early twenties made her way into the private bedroom.

Julia pushed past a tapestry, and into an alcove, where a woman was waiting. She was exotic, olive-skinned, with dark curls that fell to her waist. The two of them moved further into the shadows. 'What did he say? I was hiding.'

'And well you should, he remembers you and asked for you. The word is that you are orphaned, you are the last of your family. I'm sorry.'

'My brothers? Tomas and Anthony?'

'All dead, that's the word. You won't be rescued.'

'Ah.' Audrey turned away, but Julia took her hand.

'I said, he remembers you. He sent you here for a reason, and Gunther let you stay here to please Harald. The pig wants you, it's obvious. Don't expect to be treated well. We'll hide you as much as possible, but I sense that he will insist, eventually. Be prepared for that.' There was sympathy in Julia's eyes.

Audrey nodded briefly, and sat on the floor, her arms around her knees, her head down. She blotted out her surroundings. Her companions, however kind, were the mothers and sisters of the men who had slaughtered her pack. She lowered her head, thinking of her gentle brothers, of Tomas's laugh, and Anthony's sweet smile. Her tears flowed.

Chapter 27

Months later, hundreds of miles away from Wolf Mountain, a gaunt black wolf sniffed cautiously at the air. He could smell vegetables roasting in olive oil, rice spiced with saffron, and the rich smell of fresh beer. He whined. Winter had taken almost half his weight, his coat was a tattered wreck, and his legs were twisted and barely useful. He had a vague instinct that there was more to life than hunger and pain, but something warned him away from reaching towards those memories, something told him that a greater hurt lay there. His hunger fought against his fear of mankind, drawing him towards the scent of food and woodsmoke. He broke through scrub into a small clearing where a neat timber shack stood. Chickens panicked. He ignored them. Some rules were ingrained. He padded into the empty garden, looking for discarded food. His nose led him to a covered compost heap, and he cautiously nosed and scratched at it. He knew he would find something edible inside. Absorbed in the task, he was brutally surprised by sudden agonising pain as a heavy blow hit his head.

'That was a lucky hit,' he heard as he fell, nauseous, to the ground.

He saw three women standing over him. One held a club, and was raising it again. She paused, looking into his eyes. 'I am sorry, wolf, but we must protect the animals in our care.' She spoke as if it were a prayer. He recognised gentleness in the tone, but death in her intention. Panicked, he broke through the mental wall that divided him from his memories, and searched for the long-buried pathways that might yet save him.

The older woman brought the club up to its highest point, looking with pity at the wolf, which was starved and close to death. She looked once more into its wild yellow eyes ... then stopped, surprised, as the eyes changed in colour to a deep, beautiful brown. 'Oh, sweet mother of the world,' she said, lowering the club and kneeling next to the emaciated, torn, twisted man who now lay naked in the dirt before her.

Over the next few weeks, there was warmth, and food, and the sense that he was being cared for. For a few short days there was pain that he didn't understand, and then a deep itching in his limbs. Sensing he was safe, he took refuge in unconsciousness. Days later, his body was craving more than the liquid food that was being forced into him by the healers. He opened his eyes.

He was in a ground-floor room. There was room for a bed, and a small chest of drawers. Clothes hung from hooks on the wall, protected from the plaster by sheets of paper. He cautiously tried to sit up and, to his pleasure, realised that he was strong enough to raise himself up. He could see more in this new position, and he looked at the door, wondering if he had the strength yet to stand. He slid one leg out of bed, testing it cautiously. He saw that it was straight, which explained the pain. The women had rebroken his limbs and reset them. He decided that

Fight for the Future

the limb would bear his weight, and started to get out of bed. He stood and stretched, taking a sensual animal pleasure in the fact that he was alive and healthy.

Somewhere at the back of his mind, something wanted to be known, but he ignored it. It was the something that had almost killed him, and he didn't want to listen. He walked to the small window, seeing a well-tended garden, and a woman leaning on a spade. Looking back at him with a cautious smile, she waved. Anthony jumped back into the bed and pulled the sheet up.

The woman walked in. 'I suppose you're allowed to be shy, now that you're awake, but there's nothing I've not seen, just so that you know.' She had an easy, natural charm that relaxed him. 'I'll bring clothes for you.' He thanked her, realising that he was speaking in an Italian dialect that was unfamiliar to him. He must have absorbed it unconsciously. She blinked; she hadn't expected to be understood, this tall, hazel-eyed, brown-haired woman.

'I am Sonya,' she said.

'Anthony,' he replied, touching his chest. He blinked in surprise. 'I'd forgotten that,' he said.

'You will remember other things in time, I am sure. I will bring clothes. Come into the kitchen, we will be eating soon. You are ready to eat.' It wasn't a question.

She left, and came back with clothes. The trousers were too long, and he needed to put another couple of notches in the belt. The shirt was tight in the shoulders, and too long in the sleeves. Still, he was clothed, but barefoot. The kitchen was a large comfortable room, and he looked around hungrily, desperate for new information, new experiences. An older woman stood by the sink, peeling vegetables. Sonya introduced her as Bella. Anthony stood next to her and took up a knife and carrots, and started to scrape them. She said nothing.

'I remember nothing. Do you know me?' he said eventually.

'You are a werewolf, your name is Anthony, you were close to death at the end of winter, in wolf form. You are very beautiful. That is all we know.'

'Ah. A werewolf? I guess I knew that. You don't seem to be surprised by that.'

She shrugged. 'I've lived a long life. I know things.'

'You saved my life. Can you bring my memory back?' he said quietly.

'If you want it back. You wept, a lot. Maybe a fresh start would be better?'

'Maybe, but then how would I know how to avoid what hurt me?'

'Wisdom from one so beautiful. What would you say if I said – bread and…?'

'Butter,' he said automatically.

She nodded. 'Interesting. Black and…?'

'White.'

She continued with the game, slicing the vegetables and putting them into boiling water. 'Anthony and…?'

'Tomas,' he said, then hesitated. 'Someone else, too…'

'We'll find them. Who was Tomas? A lover? A friend?'

Anthony saw his reflection in the window. He raised his hand to his hair, pushed it back. 'My twin,' he said. He was silent.

'Do you remember?' she asked him.

'I remember that it hurts.' He said nothing else. Sonya and her daughter Maria joined them, the meal was served and eaten, and the four sat around the fire. The women told stories, and Anthony listened, quietly. Eventually, he realised that he was weeping and he didn't understand why. He excused himself and went to bed.

The following morning was fine, warm and sunny. He got up early, stripping the bed, and carrying the sheets and pillowcases to the wash house. Sonya joined him there. She looked at him questioningly.

'It's time for the girl to have her room back. I'll clean up after myself, it's the least I can do.'

'You don't have to leave,' Sonya said.

'No? That's good. I have to repay you. I will work for you. What needs to be done?'

She smiled. 'Such graciousness from a werewolf.'

'Such acceptance, from you.' They looked at each other appraisingly.

'Very well, stay. You can help around the place, but you are free to leave at any time. What we would really like as payment is information about your kind but, of course, you have forgotten much.'

'I can't tell you anything that would put us in

danger,' he said.

'I understand. But I promise that whatever you say will be kept in confidence.'

'Then I trust you, you had my life in your hands.'

'It may be painful.'

'I owe you everything, Sonya, I will tell you whatever you want to know.'

She nodded. For the rest of the day, they worked together, playing the word association game. Every so often, she would say, 'Anthony and...?' and he would say, 'Tomas'. In the early evening, he looked at her gravely. 'I think Tomas is dead.' She nodded. Later, with the girl, Maria, sitting with them, she tried again. 'Anthony and...?' He closed his eyes. He could see a photograph ... himself or Tomas, a church, a woman in white. He waved his hands in frustration.

'What is it?'

'There's a woman. I think I have, or had, a wife.'

Maria looked up mischievously. 'Anthony loves...?' she asked. Sonya frowned. 'It's not a joke,' she said, but the man looked up at the ceiling, seriously repeating the words. 'Anthony loves, Anthony loves...' Sonya and Maria looked at each other, amused. The grandmother, Bella, came in. 'Don't force it, boy. Relax. Do you remember any stories?'

He thought for a moment, then nodded. 'Yes, Pinocchio. Do you know Pinocchio?'

The women nodded. 'Tell me the story.'

He made himself comfortable, and began to tell the story of the wooden boy who longed to be a real boy. His eyes widened at one point, he was remembering something, but he carried on. At the end of the story, he looked at Bella. 'I told that story to my son. Mark. His mother is my wife, Frances. Anthony and Frances.' He smiled, and then blinked and returned to the present. 'I'll remember soon why I'm not at home with them. But for now, thank you.'

He slept in the kitchen. In the night he woke, screaming. Bella came to him, soothing him until he quieted. He stayed awake all night, staring into space. He didn't speak the next day, or the next. The women watched him warily. Eventually, taking a break from chopping wood, he turned to Sonya. 'I know why I went wolf. It doesn't hurt as much then.'

'Will you go back to that?'

'No, it's not a life. I am more than that. I have a purpose.'

'And that is?'

'Vengeance,' he said, and didn't speak again all day.

Summer came and went, autumn brought a rich harvest. Anthony worked with a will, repairing and building, gardening and hunting, ensuring that his saviours and teachers would be warm, well fed and secure against the winter to come. His memories returned, and he shared his story with the women. With the first snow, he said his goodbyes, and headed north. In the third city he came to, his early morning wolfen patrol of the darker side of town revealed the presence of a pair of White Pack scouts. He tracked them down to a cheap hotel. The following day, disguised, he listened to their conversation, and found that Harald was now the First, that Gunther and his mate were dead. He didn't change, didn't grant his prey the dignity of a fight, but waited until one of them went outside to piss, followed him, and broke his neck. He waited for the twin and did the same to him. He left a note.

'Anthony lives.'

The news came to Harald as he ate. He looked at the bloodstained note briefly. 'It's a lie,' he said. 'I killed him myself. He went over a cliff, he was broken, he was dead.'

'Something lives,' observed his twin.

'Then kill it,' the new First snapped. He left the building. Furious, he changed and climbed the mountain. At the peak he stood. He was the First, the only one, and he howled his challenge to the world.

In the night, hundreds of miles to the south, Anthony's eyes snapped open.

'Harald, I will live to watch you die.'

Acknowledgements

Thank you to Adrian, this couldn't have happened without his support.

Thank you to Hannah and Rob of Hic Dragones Press for their support and advice

Thank you to Fiction Feedback for their editing and critique work, especially Dea and Nikki.

And thank you to Ravven, for being so understanding with a first time author.